I'm an

Ka

"T

ca

warrior with a ...ley. That, and you never seem totally relaxed even when you're just making conversation. You're always scanning the room, and there's this undercurrent to you, as if you're spring-loaded."

Nick shook his head, wondering if he'd chosen the right woman to pursue. She was too observant for his comfort. "You're good."

"Not really. I have a talent for finding the one bad boy in a room full of good guys. You might even call it a curse."

Dear Reader,

I have wanted to write Kat's story since she emerged as Annie's wisecracking best friend in *Welcome Home, Daddy.* To be honest, I felt sorry for her because she had a total loser boyfriend, the latest in a long line of bad boys.

Kat is smart, beautiful and successful. Couldn't she see she deserved better? And if picking losers was a pattern for her, why didn't she simply change it?

Many of you are probably nodding and thinking, "That's just like my friend_____." Yes, we all have a friend like Kat. Heck, some of us *are* Kat. So why *do* intelligent, attractive, charming women seem to be drawn to men who are no good?

As Kat's story unfolds, I think you'll see why she needs to be needed so badly (although she covers her vulnerability with a smart-ass attitude). And I hope you'll cheer her on as she fights to let go of the past. Even as dark, intense Tony Perez will challenge her newfound courage to choose differently every step of the way.

As always, I love to hear from readers, by e-mail at carrieauthor@aol.com, or snail mail forwarded through Harlequin Books.

Yours in reading,

Carrie Weaver
www.carrieweaver.com

Once a Ranger
Carrie Weaver

HARLEQUIN®

TORONTO • NEW YORK • LONDON
AMSTERDAM • PARIS • SYDNEY • HAMBURG
STOCKHOLM • ATHENS • TOKYO • MILAN • MADRID
PRAGUE • WARSAW • BUDAPEST • AUCKLAND

ISBN-13: 978-0-373-71661-6

ONCE A RANGER

Copyright © 2010 by Carrie Weaver.

This edition published by arrangement with Harlequin Books S.A.

For questions and comments about the quality of this book
please contact us at Customer_eCare@Harlequin.ca.

® and TM are trademarks of the publisher. Trademarks indicated with
® are registered in the United States Patent and Trademark Office, the
Canadian Trade Marks Office and in other countries.

www.eHarlequin.com

Printed in U.S.A.

ABOUT THE AUTHOR

Carrie Weaver is vastly relieved that she no longer shares Kat's penchant for bad boys...or more accurately, bad men. As the mother of two young men, Carrie hopes her sons are the good guys Kat would have avoided during her loser-chasing days. When not molding the husbands of tomorrow, Carrie loves to write award-winning novels reflecting real life and real love.

Books by Carrie Weaver

HARLEQUIN SUPERROMANCE

Don't miss any of our special offers. Write to us at the following address for information on our newest releases.

Harlequin Reader Service
U.S.: 3010 Walden Ave., P.O. Box 1325, Buffalo, NY 14269
Canadian: P.O. Box 609, Fort Erie, Ont. L2A 5X3

This book is dedicated to my friend
and fellow reader Carol Cancik,
and her amazing daughter, Mary.

CHAPTER ONE

EUNICE TREADWAY DESERVED justice and Tony Perez intended to see that she got it.

Not only because Eunice's son had hired him, but also because of the there-but-for-the-grace-of-God factor. Tony would want to exact a whole lot more than justice if Will Sterling destroyed *his* widowed mother.

Tony opened his laptop and placed it on the mission-style table in the breakfast nook of his suite. Booting up, he ran through his notes; there were precious few. It wasn't that he didn't have contacts in law enforcement. As a former Texas Ranger, he had plenty. There simply hadn't been an investigation. Treadway's death had been declared a suicide, no foul play involved.

Except Tony knew better.

His cell phone buzzed. He checked the number as he went and grabbed a bottled water from the fridge under the minibar. The Phoenix Rising Resort was top of the line, even if it was in the Arizona boonies. He thumbed the button on his phone. "Hey, Teresa, how was your flight?"

"This is Brian, Teresa's husband."

Tony's shoulders tensed. She wouldn't let anyone take her BlackBerry without a fight. Even her husband.

Tony's gut told him this case could derail before it had even begun. "Yeah, we've met a couple times. Is something wrong?"

"They just took Teresa into emergency surgery. Her appendix was about to burst and the stubborn woman insisted I call you before her family." His chuckle sounded shaky. "Wanted me to tell you she's sorry she won't be able to help you with that case in Arizona."

"That sounds like Teresa." Concern for the tough ex-cop warred with the desire to punch something. "Is she going to be okay?"

"Yeah, the doctors caught it before it ruptured. A few more hours and it could have been a different story."

Tony took a deep breath, determined not to dwell on all the women who could potentially avoid destitution or worse if Will Sterling was put in jail. "Tell her to concentrate on getting better. I'm sure we'll have the chance to partner up again soon."

"I will. I gotta go call our youngest at the University of Texas."

"Take care." Clicking off his phone, Tony swore under his breath. Without Teresa for bait, luring Sterling was out of the question. Now would be the time for plan B. If he had one, that is.

There was a knock at the casita door. When he opened it, the blond, middle-aged woman who had handled his check-in smiled warmly. "I'm Linda. In case you haven't had the chance to read your brochure,

I wanted to make sure you're aware we try to keep the dining experience casual. You're invited to a welcome luncheon that starts in half an hour in the private dining room next to the Copper Dining Room. It's a small affair for the people who arrived within the past few days."

"Thank you. But I thought to get some work—"

"None of that. One of the things that sets Phoenix Rising apart from other resorts is that we encourage our guests to shake things up, meet new people, change worn-out patterns. Step outside your box, so to speak. We find that folks who form friendships with other guests are more inclined to participate in activities and are, on the whole, more satisfied with their stay here. After the welcome luncheon, our activities are more on an à la carte basis. There's a schedule on the credenza in each room."

Tony figured a con man stalking his mark wouldn't want to miss the welcome luncheon. That meant Tony couldn't miss it, either. Especially now that he was solo. And operating without a plan. "I'll be there, I promise."

"Good." She smiled warmly, clearly enjoying her job. "Will your sister arrive in time?"

"No, she just called to say her plans have changed, and she won't be able to make it at all."

"Oh, I'm so sorry. I thought it was nice for a brother and sister to vacation together. We have two sisters who always stay together at Phoenix Rising, but they're much older."

"I was looking forward to catching up with Teresa. But these things happen."

"I'm sure you'll have a wonderful stay all the same. Well, I have a few other guests to remind, so I'll see you at lunch."

Tony closed the door, calculating the pros and cons of continuing without a partner. His not-so-legal surveillance of Sterling's credit card charges had shown the man had arrived at the resort day before yesterday.

Tony had monitored Sterling's accounts regularly and this was the first time in months the weasel had gone anywhere resembling a vacation destination. Since the Treadways said Eunice had met Sterling at a resort in Texas, Tony figured he was planning to target a new victim. Smart man to vary his hunting grounds.

Even without a partner, Tony intended to stop Sterling and collect enough evidence to convince the authorities a series of felonies had been committed. Fraud, at the very least. Legally, Sterling hadn't murdered Eunice Treadway. Morally, he might as well have administered the fatal dose of pills.

Because Tony had no doubt Eunice would have continued to sing in the church choir, help shuttle her granddaughters to activities and chair a few Red Hat Lady committees if she'd never met Sterling.

KAT MONROE FELT HER reservations fade as she strolled down the gravel footpath to the lodge. The days were cooler up here around Jasper, at nearly five thousand feet, than in Phoenix, where the spring temperatures already topped one hundred degrees.

She watched birds flit from a juniper tree to manzanita shrubs. Tucking her long auburn curls behind her ear, she shielded her eyes from the glare and saw a red-tailed hawk soaring high in the sky.

Feeling the tension ease from her shoulders for the first time in months, Kat was glad she'd splurged on the pricey resort.

It seemed as if June Marsh, her best friend's mother, had been spot on in her recommendation of Phoenix Rising. Already Kat's messy life in Tempe seemed strangely removed, as if it had happened to someone else. She sighed, hoping Annie hadn't told her mother *all* the sordid details of Kat's breakup with Zach. It was humiliating to think everyone knew she'd picked the totally wrong guy again. As a thirty-two-year-old, established accountant, she should be well past picking losers. Or allowing them to choose her.

"Beautiful, isn't he?"

Kat started.

A tall, muscular man leaned against a wooden pole that supported a kerosene-style lantern, his silver hair held away from his face with a leather band. Most men couldn't carry off the gray ponytail look, but on him it seemed both masculine and…elegant, she decided. His skin was weathered from long hours in the sun, and his eyes were an unusual shade of gray.

She returned her attention to the sky. "Yes, it is. Solitary, yet powerful."

"He's got a female nesting nearby. Red-tailed hawks mate for life."

"I didn't know that."

"You're going to the luncheon?"

"Yes. Are you?"

The man pushed away from the pole and shuddered, his eyes sparkling. "Hell, no. The social stuff is more my wife's domain. You probably met Linda at check-in. I handle the art workshops and drive the excursion van. Don't miss the glassblowing exhibit after dinner tonight. It'll knock your socks off. But then again, I'm biased."

Kat raised an eyebrow, smiling at the affection in his voice. "Linda is your wife?"

"Yes. Don't look so surprised. She's not nearly as refined as she likes to pretend. And I don't always wear flannel shirts and jeans. We manage to go with the flow pretty well."

Kat realized why he seemed slightly familiar. "You're Garth Fremont. The brochure says you're famous for your blown-glass art."

He shrugged. "I've done okay."

"The next Dale Chihuly, I think Wikipedia said."

"My wife probably wrote that. She thinks I'm a genius." He winked. "That's the secret to the success of our relationship. If she ever discovers I'm just a dumb guy who likes to melt glass, I'm toast."

Kat laughed. "I seriously doubt that. But I better get to the luncheon or they'll send out a search party. Your wife said so."

"She will, too. Tenacious is her middle name. Don't forget the exhibition tonight."

"I wouldn't miss it for the world."

Kat was still smiling as she rounded the corner to the lodge, realizing it had been a long time since she'd tried something new or done anything besides what her boyfriend of the moment wanted. Now that she'd forced Zach to move out, it was time to discover what interested *her,* rather than jumping into another doomed relationship. This vacation was her chance to start a whole new way of living. The thought was both exhilarating and scary.

TONY'S STOMACH GRUMBLED as he stepped into the private dining room, a large space decorated in Southwestern style, with a stucco, beehive fireplace in one corner. The smell of food was enough to remind him he'd subsisted on coffee and power bars since hitting the road early this morning, after renting a motorcycle in Phoenix. The Harley was as much for his enjoyment as it was part of his cover playing Teresa's brother, a man facing a middle age crisis. His baggy Tommy Bahama tropical shirt was supposed to complete the impression.

He gave the buffet table a longing glance as he passed by to reach one of the two long pine tables, where several people were already gathered. He wished he'd had time to get at least the bare bones of a new plan worked out before meeting Sterling.

"Tony, why don't you sit there." Linda gestured toward the far end of the table, where there was a card with his name. There were no chairs, just a long bench on either side. "We're not formal, just trying to encourage mixing. Starting this evening, you choose your own seat in the main dining room. The round tables there seat eight—it's a good way to strike up a conversation."

"No problem."

See, I'm flexible. I can adapt to not being in charge.

He could almost hear his ex-wife, Corrine, refuting that statement in counseling, where she'd made him sound about as warm and cuddly as Attila the Hun.

"He treats me like one of his rookie officers. As if I should accept his word as the ultimate authority on everything. Having him home all the time during his… career transition…has been eye-opening."

Apparently so eye-opening that she'd asked him for a divorce after a few short sessions. No, not asked. Demanded. As if she couldn't stand to be with him one more second. Yet she still called to chat with him or ask for tips on fixing something around the house. He would never understand women. Maybe that was why he hesitated to jump back into the dating scene.

"Excuse me."

He turned to see a redhead waiting expectantly. She was medium height, her turquoise tank top revealing toned arms and plenty of cleavage. A purple skirt of lightweight crinkly fabric covered her from hips to calves.

Her eyes narrowed and he realized he was staring.

"My seat's back there." She gestured behind him, silver bangles jangling on her wrist. "I need to get by."

"Sure." He stepped to the side, wondering if he should help her maneuver around the bench. Judging from her stiff posture, he figured probably not.

Two older ladies were already seated at the table. Heads together, they whispered to each other, nodding toward the door, where a distinguished gentleman with silver hair had entered.

So far, no sign of Sterling.

Tony took his seat opposite the two women and next to the redhead. He hated having his back to the room, but didn't want to draw attention to himself by changing seats.

"Hello, ladies. I'm Tony."

"Lorraine and Lola," the one in blue said.

"We're twins," the woman in orange said. "Fraternal." As if that explained everything.

"Nice to meet you." He turned to the redhead, extending his hand.

She ignored it. "You're Tony. I heard."

He raised an eyebrow at her clipped tone. If she thought he'd been ogling her earlier, she was wrong. His ex-wife was tall, thin and blond; his taste hadn't changed much over the years. He preferred understated women, and the redhead dressed to draw attention. "According to Linda, we're supposed to be one big happy family. And your name is?"

"Kat."

"Short for Katrina?" The exotic name suited her.

"Kathleen."

"Irish?"

She rolled her eyes. "Mmm-hmm."

Then she turned her shoulder to him as the older guy sat on the other side of her. She extended her hand, her voice warm. "Hi, I'm Kat."

Shrugging off the snub, Tony glanced around. The driver's license photo he had of Sterling wasn't good quality and showed an average-looking man in his mid-thirties—thirty-six if the date of birth was to be believed. Though Tony had seen more than a few average-looking guys in the right age range at the small resort, none of them appeared to be Sterling. What if he'd already departed? Decided some larger resort provided better pickings? Or worse yet, Phoenix Rising was merely a diversion to throw someone like Tony off track, while Sterling went on to his true destination?

Wherever the man was, Tony would find him. He would track Sterling's credit card purchases as long as it took, to see where the guy holed up.

Linda approached the table. "We're waiting for three more members of your group. Please relax and take this time to get to know one another until they arrive."

Tony glanced down the table toward the three unoccupied seats. Two cards, side by side, were decorated with wedding bells. Troy and Angie Birmingham.

Unfortunately, the angle was wrong on the lone place card and Tony couldn't read it without being obvious.

He resigned himself to more waiting. Not his strong suit.

KAT WAS ACUTELY AWARE of Tony sitting next to her. It wasn't simply the fact that his arm occasionally brushed hers, or the accompanying sizzle. There was something commanding and dangerous about the man. She sensed a leashed energy, as if he was waiting for something to happen. A focused energy that reminded her of the red-tailed hawk, waiting to swoop in on a tasty morsel.

There was no way Kat would allow herself to be any man's tasty morsel. At least not until she figured out how to avoid picking jerks. And judging from Tony's earlier fixation with her breasts, he was a grade A jerk.

She heard him speaking to Lorraine and Lola, though what he was saying didn't register. But the deep, strong timbre of his voice raised goose bumps on her arms.

This was insane. He was the kind of man she knew to avoid—one who came on strong to land a woman, but barely returned a crumb of affection once the novelty wore off.

Kat was done with accepting crumbs. Next time she fell in love, she wanted the whole damn cake.

But a quick glance at his tense jaw and observant eyes had her poised to run. Or throw herself at him.

She began to stand, intent on acting on her first impulse. Because throwing herself at a virtual stranger, while satisfying in the short term, *never* ended well.

A hand brushed her shoulder. There was no accompanying zing of awareness. Sneaking another glance at Tony, Kat was surprised to see he'd turned to talk to the older man. They appeared to be deep in conversation about the merits of the Dallas Cowboys versus the Phoenix Cardinals.

"Here's my new neighbor. Kat, isn't it? We met on the shuttle to our casitas," a male voice said from behind her.

She turned to see Will standing there, a nice guy in his thirties with an easy, safe smile.

"Yes, I remember. It's good to see you again." Her tone was more effusive than she'd intended, bordering on desperate. *Damn.*

His eyes widened for a second. "Good to see you, too. You all settled in?"

"Yes. You were the one with the golf clubs, right?"

Grinning, he said, "Yes, that's me—didn't want to overdo the exercise. We'll have to talk later." He squeezed her arm and moved to his seat on the other side of the table, where he charmed Lola and Lorraine for most of the meal.

And totally ignored Kat.

How was she supposed to see if she could drum up some enthusiasm for a nice guy when he wouldn't even glance in her direction? And what did he mean by "talk later"?

With Zach, it would have meant a booty call that

turned into a three-year live-in arrangement at her place. Unfortunately, the arrangement hadn't included employment on his part.

"He's not for you." Tony's voice was low, his breath warm on the curve of her ear.

Her shoulders tensed again. Not only at his assessment, but also because she could imagine him tangled in her sheets, whispering her name in the dark.

Her best bud, Annie, would tell her to run like crazy from a man who rang her bells so insistently on the first meeting. Granted, the advice could be construed as hypocritical if her friend didn't mean so well, since Annie had slept with her husband, Drew, the evening of their blind date.

Steeling herself to make the right decision for once, Kat ignored her reawakened libido and managed a frosty glare for Tony. "I'll be the judge of what—and *whom*—is best for me. But thanks anyway."

With that, she flipped her hair over her shoulder, smacking him in the face with it. Anything to get the man to back off and stay out of her personal space.

Anything.

She managed to ignore Tony all through the meal. And then Linda broke the group into pairs for icebreaker exercises after dessert, circulating a brown paper sack. "It looks like our newlyweds have chosen to forgo the welcoming activities, which is quite understandable. But it means we have a small group. Each of the ladies needs to pick one slip of paper from the bag for your partner's name. Then follow me to the playground out back."

Tony groaned.

Kat felt the same way. Especially after she drew his name. For a woman who had recently won the lottery, she would have expected better luck. But then again, she'd had to split her winnings with four other people and contribute a healthy chunk to Uncle Sam.

Some self-destructive impulse prodded her to bait this Tony. "What's the matter? Chicken?"

In retrospect, it felt an awful lot like the impulse that had told her Zach had potential.

And she knew how well *that* had worked out.

CHAPTER TWO

THE LIGHT OF CHALLENGE in Kat's blue-green eyes made Tony reconsider inconspicuously strolling away from this kiddie playground and whatever icebreaker Linda had cooked up. Ex-Rangers did *not* do party games.

Until Kat made a clucking noise with her tongue that sounded suspiciously like a chicken.

He'd never walked away from a challenge. Folding his arms over his chest, he considered his options now that he knew for a fact Will Sterling was staying at Phoenix Rising. Being seated at dinner with the man had been a welcome stroke of luck.

An adjusted cover was essential, since Teresa wasn't here to play the role of his wealthy sister. If he appeared to be a man on the make, he would have plenty of reason to mingle with the female guests while keeping an eye on Sterling. And it might just give him the opportunity to befriend the man, one stud to another.

Hitting on Kat would be an easy way to plant that perception right away. And he wouldn't be risking his hormones getting the better of him, because she wasn't his type. It seemed like a doable solution.

Tony was distracted watching Will from the corner of his eye. He had been paired with Lola, and they were close enough that Tony could eavesdrop on their conversation.

"If I can do it, you can do it." Kat's disdain was evident as she taunted him. Tony had no idea why she'd taken an instant dislike to him, but he intended to change that, and very publicly.

"You're on, red."

"I might have to hurt you if you call me that again. My hair is auburn, for your information."

"Duly noted."

Linda walked over and handed him a bandanna. "First, I'll blindfold one person in each pair. Then I want the sighted partner to describe his or her favorite piece of play equipment from childhood, but you can't name it."

Tony raised an eyebrow, several locker room jokes coming to mind.

"Keep it clean," Kat muttered.

"That wasn't part of the instructions."

Covering his eyes with the bandanna, Linda knotted it snugly at the back of his head. "Behave yourselves. This is an icebreaker, not the battle of the sexes."

What had seemed harmless suddenly made Tony want to rip off the offending cloth. It went against every instinct to render himself helpless.

He cursed under his breath.

"I'll be gentle, I promise." Kat's whisper made him want to laugh. She was in over her head.

Tony heard Lorraine—or was it Lola?—giggle nervously as she was blindfolded. Then tell her partner she'd loved to swing as a child.

"Lorraine, you're making it too easy." Linda's tone was patient. "The idea is to give ambiguous clues. And when your partner guesses correctly or gives up, you may lead him to the appropriate equipment."

Tony was glad he could screen out Lorraine's conversation now, since she'd been paired with the older man. It was time to work on his cover and get into the spirit of competition. "What was your favorite, Kat? I have you pegged for a tomboy doing death-defying stunts on the monkey bars, showing all the boys you were better than them."

"Nice guess. My favorite required more imagination, though it was generally a solo endeavor."

"You were a loner, huh? Your clue's still too general. That could be anything on this playground, with the exception of the teeter-totter."

"Okay, my mind whirled with possibilities."

"The merry-go-round."

"Wrong again." Her voice became thoughtful, almost soft. "I could fly through the air…climb the Himilayas…."

"Swings?"

"You're not concentrating." Now it sounded as if she was smiling.

He was distracted from his purpose for a moment. "You're enjoying this, aren't you?" he accused.

"Immensely."

"Just remember, paybacks are a killer."

Her sigh brushed his cheek, smelling of peppermint.

Tony dropped his arms to his sides. "Go ahead, toy
with me all you want." He had to admit she had his
complete attention, and he was enjoying himself more
than he'd anticipated. It wasn't just the mystery the
blindfold provided. It was her in-your-face attitude.

Fingers snapped near his ear. "Pay attention. All the
other partners are already changing blindfolds. Did your
mother ever tell you not to judge a book by its cover?"
she asked.

"Yes, but I didn't listen to much she said back then.
Now I'm more willing to admit she's a truly wise
woman. How about your mom? Is she wise?"

When there was no response, he asked, "Kat?"

"I heard you. My mother has nothing to do with this.
Stay on topic, please, and listen closely. You know, you
could take a page from your mother right now."

"Huh?"

Kat let out a huff of exasperation. "Those were
clues, Einstein. Now concentrate—covers, pages, imagination…"

Irritating her was fun. She was like a pesky younger
sister. Maybe Linda had something here with the playground theme.

"Do I need to draw you a picture?"

"It would hardly be helpful, since I'm blindfolded."
He could almost imagine Kat tapping the toe of her

turquoise sandal. "Besides, you cheated. There are no books on this playground."

"I never promised to fight fair."

That's when he realized she was every bit as competitive as he was. Her laughter taunted him. But his hearing was acute and the sound revealed her location. He stepped to the right, grabbed her arm and hauled her close. Removing his blindfold, he stared into her startled eyes.

"Neither did I." He had no idea what to do now that she was so near. After sixteen years of marriage, he had little experience with flirtation.

Kat licked her lips nervously.

Reflex took over and he kissed her quickly on the mouth to give his cover some credibility. And to let her know who had really won.

She spun away and tromped a few steps across the sand before he caught up with her, grasping her shoulder. "Now who's the chicken?"

The breeze blew her hair across her eyes, but not before he saw a trace of…defeat.

He brushed the curls back from her face. "Hey, I thought we were just playing."

"That's the problem. The rules of the game always end up changing with guys like you."

She pulled free, turned and followed the path to the casitas.

He started after her, but Linda called to him.

"Let her go." She moved to his side. "I'm guessing

she needs to sort some things out. Things that have nothing to do with you or that kiss."

"I didn't mean to—"

Linda snorted. "It looked deliberate to me. Now that you know Kat's not as strong as she pretends, consider very carefully how you treat her."

Tony glanced over his shoulder to see if anyone else had noticed. They all seemed to be immersed in their own games. Though there was plenty of laughter, none seemed remotely romantic. Even Will seemed to be dividing his time equally among the sisters and the older guy, Howard.

"That was one hell of an icebreaker, lady," Tony said to Linda. "It ought to come with a warning."

She tilted her head. "In the five years we've been holding these exercises, I've never seen things transpire quite like that. You guys ought to be very interesting new additions to our guest list."

WILL GLANCED UP as Lola settled herself on the swing.

He noticed the young redhead, Kat, stalk off the playground. Her partner, Tony, started to follow, but Linda stopped him.

Odd.

Will's first impression of Kat had been that she was a nice, energetic woman. He frowned, wondering what had upset her. His instinct was to see if there was anything he could do to help, but just then Lola said, "Push me."

Her carefree, girlish tone reminded him why he did what he did. It made him feel like king of the world to bring joy to a woman. And there were so many neglected women needing his attention.

He put Kat out of his mind and focused on Lola. Placing his hand at the small of her back, he gently pushed to propel the tiny woman on the swing.

She rewarded him with a wide smile.

With the sun warm on his face and Lola's approval, Will thought it was a very good day.

AFTER LEAVING THE playground, Kat took a long walk around the grounds, avoiding the other guests. She considered leaving the resort and turning the rest of her break into a staycation at home.

But her hefty deposit was nonrefundable and the accountant in her protested the waste, despite her recent six figure lottery windfall. Especially since meals were included in the package. If she left now, she'd have to fill her empty refrigerator at home, essentially incurring food costs twice.

Besides, Tony had been out of line. She shouldn't give up her well-earned trip because he was being a jerk. Truth be told, she didn't really *want* to leave, because she'd so looked forward to her time at the resort. Leaving now smacked of defeat.

She returned to her casita determined to stick it out for at least the rest of the week. But how was she going to face the guests who had been in her group at dinner? How was she going to face Tony? By holding her head high, just as she did every other time she screwed up. At least she would never see these people again.

Cheered by the thought, she unpacked her suitcases, hastily arranging her clothing on hangers in the small closet.

The very act of unpacking brought her dad to mind, because of the hundreds of times she'd watched him unpack after a business trip. He would usually bring back a trinket for her, something he'd purchased at an airport gift shop. Kat could still recall the beautiful bottle of Chanel perfume he'd brought home when she was about eight. She had found it in his suitcase before he'd had the opportunity to unpack. She'd squealed with delight, but her mother had been furious at him for buying Kat such an expensive, grown-up gift.

Shaking her head, she realized she hadn't heard from her father recently. She opened her laptop and booted it up. Checking her sent mail folder, she saw that her last correspondence with him had been nearly a month ago. Her In folder revealed nothing new from him. Frowning, she started to worry. It wasn't like her dad to be out of touch that long. She relied on their contact, superficial as it was. In the excitement of her lottery win and vacation plans, she'd pushed it to the back of her mind.

Wazzup? The subject header for the message she composed was intentionally lighthearted. Her dad had always been particularly sensitive to anything he construed as an effort to keep tabs on him. Particularly after his divorce from her mom.

Kat constructed a few casual lines that belied her unease. After she sent the message, she wrote a quick e-mail to her mother.

There was a knock at the door, and Kat spied Will through the security peephole.

Reluctantly, she opened the door.

His grin was warm and friendly, without any underlying subtext. "I saw you leave the playground and you looked kind of upset."

It was a relief to be around an attractive man who wasn't trying to manipulate her into bed. Kat tucked a lock of hair behind her ear. "Thank you. It was sweet of you to check on me. I'm fine. Just…tired, I guess."

"That's what I figured. But I didn't want you to miss out on all the fun, so I thought I'd let you in on my favorite dorky playground toy. You know, kind of level the playing field, so to speak."

Kat returned his grin. "Would you like to come in?"

"No, I can't stay. I just wanted to make sure you were okay."

He hesitated.

"What was your favorite playground toy, Will?"

"The monkey bars."

"I imagine most boys liked that one best." A trace of sarcasm had crept into her voice. She distinctly remembered Adam Reynolds standing below and teasing her about her pink panties in the first grade.

"Probably. But for me, I wanted to help the girls who weren't strong enough to get across on their own." His eyes shone with sincerity. "I enjoyed feeling part of their sense of accomplishment."

A boy that sensitive might have been considered girlish back in the day. Probably the same logic that had Kat chasing bad boys later. She was sorry for having misjudged him. "Wow, that's really perceptive for a kid. I give you credit for being so selfless at that age."

"No, not selfless. I got satisfaction out of it." He touched her elbow lightly. "I'd better go. Maybe I'll see you at dinner tonight?"

Kat opened her mouth to say she was eating in her room, but then changed her mind. There really were good guys out there, and she couldn't allow a few bad apples like Zach and Tony to color her perception of all men. She needed to broaden her horizons, change her way of thinking.

"Yes, I'd like that."

Smiling, she closed the door and leaned against it for a moment. Maybe she could have a relationship with a nice guy like Will. Anything was possible, right?

She'd just returned to unpacking when there was another knock at her door. Kat was still smiling when she opened it. "Will—"

"Will I what?" Tony leaned in the doorway, his hands tucked in the front pockets of his jeans.

"I thought you were Will Sterling," she snapped.

He raised an eyebrow. "It appears you're recovered from your emotional outburst earlier."

Kat's hackles rose. He might as well have said she'd

had an attack of the vapors. Or the ever-popular "female problems."

"Yes, I've recovered." She started to close the door, but he stopped it with his hand.

"I came to apologize. I shouldn't have kissed you. It was…unacceptable that I acted on an impulse. I guess I didn't realize you'd be so upset."

Kat should have been relieved by his apology, but it simply made her angry. Why did the macho guys always think she was just waiting for their attention? Not that Tony was strictly macho. He was also confident, good-looking and charismatic. The kind of man who didn't need a woman.

Frowning, he said, "I was out of line. I guess I got too caught up in the spirit of fun. I hope you'll let me make it up to you later."

"Not hardly. Why should I? You made me sound like a hysterical female."

"Because you're intrigued, even though you won't admit it."

He winked and walked away, whistling as he went.

CHAPTER THREE

TONY SHOOK HIS HEAD as he walked the perimeter of the buildings. Glancing around as if enjoying the desert landscaping, he located casita number eighteen, right next door to Kat. He'd overheard Will tell Lola his suite number as he'd pushed her on the swing.

Tony didn't like Sterling being close to the mercurial Kat Monroe, but he doubted she was the con man's mark. Too young, too sharp and not nearly as liquid in assets as beer heiresses Lola and Lorraine.

He nodded at a middle-aged couple strolling hand-in-hand in the opposite direction. After glancing over his shoulder to make sure they'd walked around the bend, he veered off the path and went behind the casitas to check egress. Yes, there was a glass Arcadia door leading to a private patio, bordered by a three-foot stucco wall. Several large windows also faced the back. If worse came to worst, Sterling's suite could be accessed without much trouble.

Quickly returning to the path, Tony was relieved to find no one in sight.

He categorized the flora and fauna as he walked, noting many plants similar to those in Texas. A few minutes later, he came upon two large stucco buildings. One had a discreet bronze marker saying Art Studio, the second Athletic Facilities.

As he approached, he saw a familiar redhead jog around a curve in the path. Tony stepped off into a stand of brush so she wouldn't see him.

When she entered the gym, he headed back to his casita by the most direct path, grateful he'd brought plenty of workout clothes.

What better time than now to check out the exercise facilities?

KAT STARTED TO SWEAT in the short run from her casita to the gym. The higher elevation made her work harder.

Good. She intended to sweat Zach and Tony right out of her system. Exercise had a habit of taking the edge off her anger, too. Hadn't she sworn off drama for the duration of her trip? Hopefully, she would return home in two weeks reenergized, with a whole new attitude. She was so tired of being mad. And even worse, feeling like a victim.

The blast of air-conditioning was a welcome reprieve when she entered the gym. The large, open space was light and airy, with state-of-the-art equipment. Nothing shabby here, and enough variety for the average fitness enthusiast. Since the resort was small—around fifty casitas and rooms—she wondered if the owners used Phoenix Rising as a tax write-off. Though the rates were steep, it would still be difficult to turn a profit.

Especially since Phoenix Rising hosted a camp for at-risk kids for a month during the off season.

Her breathing slowed as she checked out the whiteboard for class information. Tai chi might be relaxing, but Pilates was probably more in line with what she needed to keep her butt from sliding down her thighs.

"Hi, I'm Brooke." A svelte blonde with rock-hard abs and toned biceps extended her hand. She looked to be all of twenty. "I'm the fitness instructor and also provide personal training."

"I'm Kat." She'd already established a workout that suited her, though the blonde would probably think it wimpy. "Looks like you've got a pretty good setup."

"My mom and dad believe in a balanced lifestyle, and we try to provide that to our guests while they're here."

"Your mom and dad? Linda and Garth Fremont?"

"Yes. I'm working for them while I finish up my bachelor's degree online."

"Linda doesn't look old enough to have a daughter your age."

Brooke laughed, showing off straight white teeth and a dimple.

Kat wanted to hate her, but couldn't.

"I'll tell Mom you said that. It'll make her day. Do you want me to show you around?"

"You have some of the machines and weights I've worked with at my neighborhood gym. I may touch base with you later, if that's okay?"

"Absolutely. Enjoy your workout."

"I will," she murmured, trying not to notice that everything on Brooke was perky. Kat decided to spend a little extra time on her glutes today.

Inserting her earbuds, she lost herself in the routine of warming up on the treadmill, then moving on to the weight machines. She switched her music to a favorite heavy metal track as motivation. As Green Day's latest hit energized her, she focused on her breathing and her reps.

When she opened her eyes several minutes later, she was startled to see Tony looming over her. He was every bit as ruggedly handsome upside down as right side up.

She reluctantly removed her ear buds. "How long have you been watching me?"

"Not long," he drawled in a Tommy Lee Jones way, probably aware it was sexy as hell.

"You're breaking my concentration."

"Sorry." He seemed anything but sorry as he handed her a sheet of paper. "Brooke asked me to give you this revised class schedule. She said the testosterone's getting thick in the kickboxing class and she'd love for you to attend. I hear it really works the glutes."

Kat couldn't decipher his deadpan tone. Was that a lame come-on? Or was her butt genuinely that saggy? Then a truly horrifying thought occurred to her. What if he was drumming up business as a way to curry favor with the svelte Brooke?

He grinned, sauntering off.

Glaring daggers at his retreating back, Kat was

determined about one thing. No kickboxing for her. Unless it meant kicking *his* ass...

AFTER SHOWERING AND shaving, Tony arrived at the dining room a few minutes late, a fact that irked him. He prided himself on being early.

Linda smiled as she came around the hostess stand. "Even though you're now in the main dining room, I've taken the liberty of assigning seating one last time. Howard's great-grandchild was born today and he's cutting his stay short to return home. I thought the guests who'd met him might want to wish him well. Lola and Lorraine in particular seemed quite attached to him. I'm afraid he's the only single man in his age group here right now."

"Sure, no problem." And it wasn't. Tony would be seated at the same table as Sterling.

"Follow me." Linda led him to the appropriate table. The Southwestern decor was the same as in the Copper Dining Room, but this space was much larger, with round tables and crisp white tablecloths. He figured it probably maxed out at a hundred people, though not all the tables were occupied.

Gesturing at an empty chair, she said, "Right over there between Lola and Lorraine."

He raised an eyebrow.

Leaning close, she whispered, "I split them up to encourage them to mingle more with other guests. They spend plenty of time together as it is. Bicker like crazy, but seem devoted all the same."

Nodding, Tony took his seat. He located Sterling, sitting on the other side of Lola. And on Sterling's right, Kat.

She nodded, her gaze frosty.

Her ambivalence would work perfectly for Tony. He could pursue her without having to worry about actually catching her. He had his ethical limits.

The waiter served his salad, which Tony, never a fan of green leafy stuff, moved around with his fork. Vegetables had their place, but he preferred something more…substantial.

He felt someone come up behind him and he turned his head to find Brooke leaning close. "Thank you for helping me out today," she murmured.

"It was nothing." He felt the tips of his ears burn, and hoped no one noticed. It wasn't as if he was unaccustomed to women hitting on him. They did, fairly regularly. Not that Brooke was hitting on him. She'd told him about her boyfriend, who wanted to become a cop, and Tony had given her some Web sites to help him prepare for the exams.

No, his discomfort had more to do with Kat's smirk, as if he'd confirmed some suspicion she had.

Sterling complimented Lola on her dress, and she preened like a junior high girl at her first dance. Lorraine, however, was unusually quiet, studying Sterling when he wasn't looking.

Tony wondered if one of the older women would become Sterling's next victim. He would have to find out more about them.

Howard leaned close to Lorraine. "My granddaughter's husband sent me this picture of the baby." He opened his phone and fiddled with the buttons for a minute or so, until he pulled up the photo. "See? Strapping boy."

"He's gorgeous," Lorraine gushed.

"Beautiful," Lola concurred, passing the phone to Sterling.

"Um, great kid." Will handed it on to Kat.

Tony watched her eyes cloud for a moment before she smiled. "He's great, Howard. You have every right to be proud."

She slid the phone toward Tony, past the two empty spaces where the elusive newlyweds were supposed to sit.

Picking it up, Tony saw a newborn with eyes squeezed tightly shut and brown fuzz for hair. "Handsome boy, just like his great-grandpa."

"Always nice to know," Sterling said, "there's family to carry on after we're gone."

"Our father would have dearly loved for Lorraine and I to have lots of children, but it wasn't to be." Lola's lips trembled, but Will smiled at her and she rallied.

Tony sipped from his water glass, acting unconcerned with the interplay.

A waiter brought bread baskets and set them on the table, before moving on to the next.

Sterling grabbed one, peeling back the napkin to present the rolls to Lola with a flourish. "Ladies first."

"Why, thank you, Will. You're a lovely boy."

"You're a lovely woman." When she had chosen her roll, he selected one for himself. "Your husband must be very proud."

"I've never married. I had a fiancé once, but he left me at the altar for another woman."

Sterling touched her arm. "I'm sure he was sorry later. He had to have been an idiot."

"He was killed during a thunderstorm, drowned in a flash flood. His wife was left a penniless widow. Of course, I would not have been penniless. And I might have had children to carry on the family business."

Tony watched Sterling closely, but the only emotion he saw was concern for his dinner companion as Will said, "Your father probably appreciated having two daughters. I'm sure he knew you would take care of the business. Didn't you say you're in the restaurant trade?"

"We own Nash Brewery."

"Oh, yes, that's it." Will turned to Howard. "And you were a postal carrier, weren't you?"

"For forty years. I invested well before I retired."

"And what is it you do, Will?" Kat asked.

"I'm a life coach. I help people develop positive patterns to become more successful in life and relationships."

"That sounds fascinating," she said. "Much more interesting than the number crunching I do. I'm a CPA."

Tony almost did a double take. Kat seemed more the wild, artistic type.

"Kat, dear, tell them about your lottery win. I'm sure everyone will be most entertained. It's such a cute story," Lorraine said.

Everyone turned to Kat and waited expectantly.

She hesitated.

"Come on, Kat. You've got to tell us now," Sterling prodded.

"Well, it happened about a month ago. I'd…broken up with my boyfriend and I have this breakup tradition. I buy lottery tickets, and the numbers I use are all the special numbers from the relationship. Our first date, his birthday, my birthday, things like that."

Lola sighed, obviously a dreamer. "How tragic. And romantic."

"It gets better," said Lorraine. "Tell them the rest."

"I bought tickets the day Zach moved out. And, well, I won with our special numbers."

Clapping her hands, Lola pronounced, "Then Zach will come back to you. It was meant to be."

From the way Kat had said her boyfriend's name, Tony suspected she was well rid of him.

"More likely it means you did the right thing to kick the guy to the curb. Kind of like the universe smiling on your decision," he said.

Kat selected a roll, taking her time tearing off a piece and slathering it with butter. "Fate is overrated. I think it means the little white balls simply dropped in that order."

"Lorraine was right, it's a great story." Sterling beamed at Kat, his gaze warm. "We're honored to have a millionaire in our midst."

"Three millionaires," Lola crowed.

Lorraine elbowed her sister, giving her a meaningful look.

Lola didn't seem to notice. Tony wondered if she'd always been so guileless, or if a small stroke at one time had affected her judgment. Or it could even be the early stages of Alzheimer's.

Kat held up two fingers. "Just a pair. After the jackpot was split among five winning tickets, and Uncle Sam took his chunk, I received a lot less than people think." She blotted her mouth with her napkin. "Don't get me wrong, it's a fabulous thing and I'm extremely grateful. But I'm not likely to join the millionaires' club anytime soon."

"Still, it's a nice windfall." Lorraine leaned forward. "If you need the name of a top-notch investment firm, I can refer you to the one we use. Our advisor has been very helpful in growing and safeguarding our assets. A single woman can never be too careful."

"No brothers to help?" Sterling asked her. "Or nieces and nephews?"

"No." Lorraine's voice was tinged with loss. "We had a younger sister, but she died as an infant."

Tony could almost see the wheels turning in Sterling's head. Him selecting a new victim meant Tony might find evidence. But it also meant the Nash sisters would get hurt.

Will leaned forward. "Tony, what is it you do?"

"I'm a security consultant."

"I bet that's fascinating work. Foiling corporate espionage and all that?"

"Yes. But because of the spread of identity theft, more and more of my work is securing client information. It's become a real liability issue."

"I can imagine. I've been meaning to update the security software on my computer to make sure my client files don't fall into the wrong hands. Do you have a card?"

Removing his wallet from his back pocket, Tony pulled out a pseudo business card. "I'll give you a discount, since you're a friend."

"Great. I'll call you after I get back from vacation." Sterling slid the card into the breast pocket of his button-down shirt.

The thought of getting his hands on Sterling's computer practically made Tony salivate. It was the easy kind of lie that cons used to bond with people, but still…

Lorraine and Lola regaled them with tales of their youth until their meals arrived.

Tony had selected the top sirloin with mixed seasonal vegetables from the Phoenix Rising garden. A footnote on the menu had indicated guests' help in the garden was always welcome.

"These vegetables are wonderful," Kat exclaimed. "Why can't I cook them this way?"

"My guess is they taste so good because they're

fresher than a lot of grocery store produce," he answered.

"You cook?" She seemed intrigued in spite of herself.

"Not much, but I'm learning. My ex-wife was big on buying locally grown, organic. I don't cook when I'm working long hours, but now that I have my own business I sometimes have slow times."

She tried to turn to Sterling, but he was deep in conversation with Lola.

"Do you garden?" Tony asked Kat.

"No, I've always been busy, too. But I'm realizing just how close to burning out I was. It's not good for me to work sixty hours a week and never take vacations…." Shaking her head, she said, "I don't know why I told you that. My life is fine the way it is."

Tony was curious. On one hand, Kat seemed independent, with a streak of wildness, on the other she was solid and dependable.

He sipped his wine. "Sure, we all think our lives are fine right before we crash and burn." He winced at the bitterness in his voice. Where in the hell had that come from? Striving for a more casual tone, he asked, "If there was one thing you could change about your life, what would it be?"

Man, he'd been spending too much time listening to marriage counselors.

She hesitated. "I'd quit expecting other people to make me happy. I'd do more things that were good for me, without considering what anyone else thought. All those activities I've dreamed about over the years, but said I didn't have time for. Maybe learn to cook. Grow a few vegetables and flowers in a garden. I don't know, it's something to consider."

"Sounds like a win-win proposition." He shook his head. "Don't tell my ex I said that, though. She was always after me to have more balance in my life. Less work, more play and relaxation."

"You don't impress me as the relaxed type."

The waiter came and refilled their water glasses. Tony was tempted to elbow the guy out of the way so as not to lose the headway he'd made with Kat. At the same time, he tried to follow the conversation between Will and the sisters.

After Kat thanked the waiter, she turned to Tony, raising an eyebrow. "Well, am I right? You're an adrenaline junkie?"

"Hey, I can be as relaxed as the next guy," he protested. "But when I'm involved in something, I'm involved one hundred percent."

"I can relate." She picked up her water glass and stared into it for a moment before taking a sip. "I'm that way in my relationships. I've been told it leaves very little room for the other person…to contribute."

The last thing Tony wanted to do was contemplate his failed marriage and whether he'd *contributed* enough. Because, hands down, Corrine had done the lion's share. At the time it hadn't been so obvious. Or maybe he simply hadn't wanted to know.

Shaking his head, he forced his thoughts to the

present. "So what made you think I'm an adrenaline junkie?"

She nodded at his feet. "The biker boots. And I saw you in the lobby carrying a helmet. I figure you're a weekend warrior with a Harley. That, and you're always scanning the room as you talk, plus there's this undercurrent to you, as if you're spring-loaded."

Tony wondered if he'd chosen the right woman to pursue. She was too damn observant for his comfort. Never a good thing in undercover work.

"You're sharp," he said.

"Not really. I simply have a talent for finding the one bad boy in every room. You might even call it a curse."

CHAPTER FOUR

KAT COULDN'T BELIEVE she'd called Tony a bad boy. Or admitted her Achilles' heel.

She watched out of the corner of her eye as he cut a piece of steak, speared it with his fork and shoveled it into his mouth.

He wiped his mouth with the cloth napkin and asked, "You had this talent long?"

"Since puberty."

A smile twitched his lips. "I see."

"No, I don't think you do. I've decided to use my talent, as you call it, for good rather than evil. I've promised myself I'll run like hell next time I zero in on the bad boy."

"Darlin'," he drawled, "you're mistaken about one thing. I'll admit to my share of bad moments. But I haven't been considered a boy by a beautiful woman since *I* reached puberty. I'm one hundred percent *man*."

If it was coming from another guy, Kat might have challenged this cocky statement. But she had no doubt Tony could live up to his self-anointed title given half a chance.

She resisted the urge to fan herself with her napkin and gulp her ice water. The room temperature had to have ratcheted up at least twenty degrees.

Tony leaned back in his chair and sipped his wine, all confident male.

Raising an eyebrow, she said, "While bad boys have a certain amount of charm, bad men are downright creepy. If they're not in jail, that is. Then they're wards of the state. And if they're bad *old* men, they're just pathetic."

He laughed, showing straight white teeth and a dimple. His brown eyes sparkled.

Kat caught her breath, surprised by the intensity of the connection she felt with him. It was almost tangible, and transcended the fact that she couldn't stand him.

A high-pitched laugh from the other side of the table reminded her they weren't alone.

"Aren't you two just the cutest thing," Lola said, still laughing. She reached across Will to jostle her sister's arm. "They remind me of that bartender, Sam, and the cocktail waitress, Diane. All that frustrated banter when you know they just want to tear each other's clothes off."

Lorraine reluctantly turned from Howard. "Who? Sam and Diane from *Cheers?*"

"We have our own Sam and Diane—Tony and Kat. Isn't it fun?"

Kat felt her cheeks warm and wished the ground would swallow her up. She'd found Lola's almost child-like views charming until this moment. It made her wonder if Lorraine was the older twin by seconds, and as such, had always kept an eye out for her younger sibling.

A responsibility Kat had been spared when her baby sister, Nicole, had gone to live with their mom after the divorce. They might have had a stronger bond if they'd at least lived in the same household.

Tony, on the other hand, seemed to be enjoying the attention. "Now, Lola, we were only kidding around. You're going to embarrass Kat. See, she's blushing."

The older woman leaned forward, her voice a stage whisper. "That's because she wants you."

Just then a commotion at the other side of the table had Will jumping to his feet.

"Oh, my," Lola said.

"I'm so sorry." He dabbed ineffectively at her lap. Her wine goblet was overturned on the table in front of her.

"I have to change my skirt and treat this stain before it sets."

"I'm such a klutz. Let me walk you to your casita, Lola. It's the least I can do."

Kat could have kissed him. She suspected he had created the diversion to save her embarrassment.

Lorraine gazed longingly at Howard for a few seconds before she stood. "I'll walk my sister back to her room."

"No need to bother yourself. I'm the one who made the spill. I should make it right," Will stated.

"Really, it's—"

"I insist. Sit down and enjoy your dinner. I'll ask the waiter to keep our plates warm in the kitchen."

Lorraine slowly sat. "I would hate to miss a moment of Howard's going away dinner. Are you sure you don't need me, Lola?"

"Positive," she replied. There was a spring in her step as she left the table with Will, who cupped her elbow.

Kat turned and noticed Tony was watching them, too, his eyes narrowed.

TONY LEANED BACK in his chair as dinner was cleared, trying to appear relaxed when he was itching to find out what Sterling was up to.

Before they could begin to break up, Linda came by their table. "I wanted to invite you all to a special demonstration in the art studio in twenty minutes. In honor of his new great-grandson, Howard has commissioned my husband to create a glass sculpture to present to the proud parents. Garth won't allow an audience when he's working on the actual piece, but he's going to make a special ornament to commemorate the baby's birth. I'm sure Howard would love it if you would join him. Garth might take some requests from the audience, too, if you have special occasions coming up. Cake and coffee will be served afterward."

"Oh, dear, Lola wouldn't want to miss it." Lorraine's hand was tucked in Howard's arm, her dilemma clear.

"How about if you two go ahead," Tony suggested,

"and I stop by your suite to tell her? That way you won't miss any of the demonstration."

"Thank you, Tony. We're in casita number eight."

"No problem."

Kat eyed him speculatively. "What, not an art lover? Trying to duck out of the demonstration?"

"On the contrary." He opened the double door for her. "But Lola's been gone an awfully long time. I'm kind of worried about her."

"She's with Will, so I'm sure she's fine. But it's… unexpectedly nice of you. And should set Lorraine's mind at ease."

He couldn't help but laugh. "Yep, that's me—nice, pathetic, old bad man."

"No, you haven't quite reached the old and pathetic stage. That's what makes you so dangerous."

Kat thought he was dangerous? He'd obviously failed in his attempt to seem harmless. Her powers of observation might end up being a problem down the road. He would have to remember not to underestimate her. "That's a relief. Save me a seat?"

"Maybe." She rose. "Or maybe not. I'd hate for you to think I was predictable."

"No worries about that."

They left the restaurant in a group.

"I'll go check on Lola," Tony called to Lorraine as he took the side path that looped around to her unit.

He was halfway there when he saw Lola and Sterling headed in his direction. Covering the ground between them, he said, "There you are. Linda wanted me to tell you that there's a special demonstration tonight in the art studio, followed by cake for Howard."

"Thanks for letting us know." Sterling tucked Lola's hand in his arm. "You go on ahead. That way you won't miss the start."

"I'll walk with you two. I don't mind missing a few minutes." He wanted to see how the con man worked. Maybe Sterling would let something important slip.

"Nonsense, Tony. These old legs of mine move too slowly," Lola said. "Will promised to be my devoted servant for the rest of the evening."

A devoted servant with his hand in her pocket.

But Tony didn't want to raise Sterling's suspicions by overstaying his welcome. "If you're sure?"

Will smiled. "Positive. I'll see that this lady arrives safe and sound."

"Okay, I'll tell Lorraine you're on your way."

Lola waved him off as she started telling Sterling a story about the time she'd met an Arab prince.

Tony turned and followed the path to the studio, catching up to Kat on the way. She stood in the path, gazing up at the sky.

"What'd I miss?"

"Bats." Her voice was tinged with awe. "You can see them in the moonlight."

"What's so fascinating about bats?"

"We don't have many in Phoenix. It amazes me that things can change so much only a hundred miles from the city. I saw a red-tailed hawk this afternoon."

"You need to come to Texas then. We have more

hawks and bats than you'd ever believe. You grew up in Phoenix? Let me guess—you were a rebel in high school?"

She shook her head and started to walk down the path again. "No way," she said over her shoulder. "I was president of the chess club, then did a stint in debate. The science club, too."

He caught up to her in two strides. "You? A nerd?"

"I preferred to think of myself as an intellectual."

"A fiery intellectual then."

"Save the compliments for someone who cares."

"Ouch. I was sincere."

Her tone was light when she said, "That's what all the bad men say. Where in Texas are you from?"

Grasping her arm, he pulled her to a stop. "Shh. See, over there under that cedar tree? It's a mama javelina and her baby out for an evening snack."

"Wha— Oh, I see," she whispered. "They're so dark I almost couldn't make them out—smaller than pigs I've seen at the fair. How sweet."

"Yes, but those mamas get mean if you get too close to the babies."

They started walking again and the javelinas trotted off into the brush.

"You never answered my question about where you're from. Are there javelinas in Texas?"

"I was born and raised in San Antonio. And yes, we have javelinas, too."

"You've never wanted to live somewhere else?"

He shrugged. "My family's there, my friends.… And an ex-wife."

"Why am I not surprised you're divorced? How long were you married?"

"Sixteen years." He glanced around as they walked. "No kids, though."

"Did you want kids?"

"Enough about me. Have you been married? Want kids?"

She hesitated, then gave him a withering glance. "Don't bother trying to get me to talk about myself so I'll let my guard down. I'm not interested in you, so sharing my history would only be a waste of time."

"Ouch. Prickly much?"

She snorted. "Only with assholes."

He threw back his head and laughed. Damn, he enjoyed sparring with her. She tried so hard to compensate for her vulnerability. He'd already figured out that her family and babies were sore topics for her.

The baby thing wasn't hard to figure out. He could almost hear her maternal clock ticking from a couple feet away.

What was it about her family she didn't want him to know? Tony filed the question away for future reference.

"Laugh all you want, just leave me alone. I'll wait for Lola."

CHAPTER FIVE

KAT COULD NOT BELIEVE Tony's arrogance.

He'd called her prickly simply because she didn't fall for his obvious come-ons. Because she saw through him and understood he was the type of man she should avoid.

Sixteen years? A man married that long should seem solid enough. Except that Tony hadn't said he'd been *faithful* for all that time. Or that he'd been a decent husband.

Take her dad, for instance. She remembered her mother yelling at her father after his return from a business trip to Vegas. She'd been sorting his laundry and found a slip of paper with the name and phone number of a woman.

It was only the second time Kat had heard her parents fight. They'd announced their divorce a short time later.

A familiar sense of loss hit her hard. Her eyes misted as she wondered if that fight had marked the end of their family as she'd known it. And wondered why the memory had been buried all this time....

"Dear, is everything all right?"

She turned to see that Lola and Will had caught up with her.

"Oh, um, yes, everything's fine. I…got something in my eye. I'll be along shortly."

"We don't want to leave you out here by yourself, do we Will?"

He glanced at the studio, then grinned. "No, we don't."

That's when Kat remembered they hadn't even eaten dinner yet.

"I'll be fine. It's perfectly safe out here. You two go along, I'll be there in a minute." She stepped off the path to let them by.

"If you're sure…" Lola's gate was stiff and slow. It would have been hard for her to stand for very long. It had been sweet of her to offer, though.

"Positive."

Linda was waiting inside the door when Kat arrived a few minutes later. "We're out back near the kilns. Unfortunately, we have to keep the studio doors locked because some kids from town vandalized Garth's work last year. It was so sad. They smashed several pieces to bits." She locked the front door behind them and led the way through the studio.

"Oh, how horrible," Kat said.

Glancing around, Kat was immediately impressed by Garth's art, displayed on lit pillars of different heights and shapes. There were large bowls with fluted edges in greens and blues. A more whimsical one had yellow polka dots. The pieces seemed to shift and flow with the light, as if they were undersea creatures. It had to be an optical illusion.

"I haven't seen too much handblown glass, but even I can tell his work is special."

"Yes." Linda fairly beamed. "You'll be even more amazed when you see all the work that goes into a piece. But Garth makes it seem effortless."

"I'll have to come back and look more closely another time."

"Please feel free. The hours are posted near the front door. There are also several pieces for sale in the gift shop."

The temperature rose at least ten degrees when they walked outside. Two large kilns were situated on a detached, covered patio, the roof and poles of which were made of some sort of metal. It was a strictly utilitarian area, in contrast to the display inside.

Kat recognized Garth from meeting him earlier, when he'd pointed out the hawk to her. The artist was perched on a tall metal stool in the center of the courtyard. He wore faded jeans and a long-sleeved chambray shirt.

To her right was an assortment of metal chairs arranged to make an impromptu viewing area, like some ragged, independent theater production.

"Go ahead and sit down," Linda directed, pointing. "There's a chair over there."

Kat stifled a groan. She might have known, the only seat left in the house would be right next to Tony. Could this evening get any better?

She squeezed by several people she didn't know to get to the seat.

But Tony didn't even seem to notice, he was so focused on Garth.

TONY WAS BARELY AWARE of Kat sliding into the seat next to him. He'd been refining a short-term plan for his investigation while watching the glass artist work his magic.

Sterling and Lola had arrived a few moments ago. Lorraine had saved only one seat for her sister, so Will had been relegated to sitting next to the newlyweds. If he was irritated, he didn't show it. He came across as a laid-back, genuine kind of guy.

Except Tony knew better.

He'd decided against breaking into Sterling's casita unless there was no other option. Becoming buddies with the con man seemed his best bet for gaining information and staying on the right side of the law. And the law was still important to him.

Garth's demonstration interrupted his thoughts, as the artist explained the variables in temperature, air pressure and materials. Tony soon realized why each piece was unique.

It was fascinating to watch the man twirl molten glass on a long tube while his twenty-something male assistant blew into the other end of the tube. Before Tony's eyes, a vaselike shape emerged, but not apparently to Garth's satisfaction.

He opened the door to the kiln and placed the vase, tube still attached, inside, rotating it skillfully. Seconds later, he withdrew it and resumed the process.

"Amazing," Tony murmured.

"Not nearly as amazing as your ego." Kat shifted, crossing her arms over her chest.

"What's my ego got to do with it?" He didn't look her way. The glass cooled so quickly Garth had to work at a rapid pace.

"How dare you call me a bitch," she whispered.

"I didn't call you that."

"You might as well have. *Prickly* is the same thing."

He risked a glance in her direction. He'd learned to recognize a storm brewing as a kid, when his normally smiling mother had worn a similarly tight expression. Usually because she was pissed at his dad, but would snap at Tony for leaving the milk on the counter or tracking in mud. He didn't mess with her when she was in that state. "You aren't really upset about that, are you? There's something else."

"Of course not."

He sighed, frustrated that she wouldn't own up, but added, "You may be right." That was the only helpful phrase he'd picked up in counseling.

Kat snorted. But at least she was quiet after that.

Still, he felt as if he'd failed some important test. Kind of like retiring from the Rangers at Corrine's request and being served with divorce papers a month later. He'd done what she'd asked, sacrificed a career he'd loved, but it still hadn't been enough.

"Mr. Birmingham," Garth asked, "what's your favorite color?"

The young husband, who had finally joined the group, managed to stop kissing his blond bride long enough to reply, "Blue."

"Ah, I can see that. Your wife has blue eyes."

She giggled.

The groom raised her hand to his lips and kissed her palm, adoration smoldering in his eyes.

Kat made a strangled noise.

"What's wrong now?" Tony whispered.

"How can they be so young and so in love?"

He shrugged. "We all were, once...."

Garth did his thing with the molten glass while everyone watched.

But despite Kat's relative silence, Tony had a hard time concentrating, his attention drawn by Sterling and the need to figure out the man's next move. Was Lola his target? How would he manage to separate her from not only her sister, but her trust fund?

"A gift for you, from the staff at Phoenix Rising." Garth presented the newlyweds with two beautiful champagne glasses in swirls of blue layered upon clear glass.

Impressed and clearly touched, the pair thanked Garth. A few minutes later, they ducked out hand-in-hand. It didn't take a brain surgeon to realize they would fall back into bed the minute they arrived at their casita....

Kat bumped Tony in the arm as she shifted in her seat.

"Do you ever sit still?" he asked, irritated that the newlyweds made him nostalgic.

"I can sit still fine when I enjoy the company." Her sniff told him she wasn't likely to forget his prickly remark.

WHEN KAT ARRIVED in the dining room for breakfast the next morning, she scanned the room and found Tony's dark presence at a table on the left. So she swerved right.

Even though the other half of the large room had been closed off by a temporary divider, she felt conspicuous and exposed. It appeared that far fewer people showed up for breakfast than for dinner.

"Is anyone sitting here?" she asked at a table where she knew no one.

"You are." A middle-aged man with a bad toupee snickered.

His wife glared at her as if she'd propositioned him.

Kat slid into the seat and tried to make small talk with her companion on the left. But the elderly woman was extremely hard of hearing and she soon tired of shouting.

The server came by and took her drink request, then directed her to the buffet table along the far wall.

She lined up behind two girls who appeared no older than eighteen. They wore bikini tops and sarong skirts, their bare, tan legs going on forever.

Kat felt old and frumpy in her white shorts and teal short-sleeved shirt. She loved bright colors and loose, flowing clothes, but they were impractical at an accounting firm, so she had only a few outfits in which she could indulge her free-spirited side, as her friend Annie called it.

"Good morning," a man said close to her ear.

Judging from the way the hair on the back of her neck stood up, she knew who it was without looking. "Morning."

"Are you ignoring me?"

She turned to face Tony, who looked athletic and alpha in cargo shorts and a black T-shirt that revealed impressive pecs and biceps, offset by a truly fine set of abs. Why he'd been hiding all those magnificent muscles under a tentlike beach shirt yesterday she couldn't imagine.

Great, just what she needed. Not only did the man exemplify the qualities she wanted to avoid, but he also had a body to die for.

"Why would I be ignoring you?"

"Because you haven't yet realized what a charming companion I can be."

Kat snorted. "Oh, please. *Charming* is a stretch."

"Devastatingly handsome?" He selected a plate and silverware.

Kat raised her chin. "How did we get on the subject of your purported magnificence?"

"I don't know." He shrugged. "I simply told you good morning."

"Good morning." And with that, she turned her back on him, determined not to be tempted.

"Have a nice day, Kat," he murmured as he strolled to the other side of the buffet table.

She felt his gaze the whole time she was filling her plate. Consequently, she was so nervous that her food choices were less than…balanced. French toast, pancakes, bacon, hash brown potatoes…and the Belgian waffles looked heavenly.

With a sigh, Kat knew she would be spending a lot of time at the gym.

WILL SURVEYED THE dining room, swearing under his breath. He'd overslept, and now he probably wouldn't be able to snag a seat near Lola.

As luck would have it, he saw her at a table near the buffet, Lorraine ever present beside her. But the chair on Lola's left was unoccupied.

Will smiled, sauntering over to their table. "Good morning, ladies. Is this seat taken?"

Lola glanced up at him, her cheeks rosy this morning, whether from makeup or his presence he couldn't tell. Either way, he knew his attention brought her joy. Yes, it was good to be him today.

She placed her hand on his arm. "We'd be delighted to have you sit with us. Wouldn't we, Lorraine?"

Her sister puckered her lips as if she'd sampled one of the lemon slices arranged on a cut glass plate in the middle of the table. "I suppose you might as well sit there, since no one else is." Her narrowed gaze as much as told him she would be watching him.

Lorraine could prove to be a problem. It wouldn't be the first time he'd had to circumvent pushy relatives to work his magic. Some people just couldn't stand to see others happy. And he suspected Lorraine was one of them.

Old hag.

He gave her his best smile. "Thank you. Great morning, isn't it."

She spooned up her oatmeal.

Unfolding his napkin, he placed it over the back of his chair to signify the seat was taken.

"May I get either of you anything from the buffet?"

"No, thank you," they said in unison. Lola giggled. Lorraine frowned.

"A Danish or cinnamon roll? You both look as if you need to be careful not to get too thin."

Lola giggled again.

Lorraine's frown deepened.

"I'll bring each of you back something sweet." He held Lola's gaze a moment longer.

"No, thank you." Lorraine's voice brooked no argument.

"If you're sure…?"

"Very sure."

He walked to the buffet table and made selections designed to help him stay in top shape. He also took a large cinnamon roll for Lola. As for Lorraine, there wasn't any ground glass or arsenic available.

CHAPTER SIX

ON HER WAY BACK from her second trip to the buffet table, loaded down with fruit, Kat noticed Lorraine, Lola and Will and threaded her way through the tables toward them.

Kat greeted the three, admiring the sisters' cropped jeans, linen camp shirts and matching vests. "You look very outdoorsy this morning."

"Yes, there's a hike around the grounds at ten." Lorraine's eyes sparkled with anticipation.

"I'm not sure I should go." Lola twisted her napkin. "I'll just slow everyone down."

"Nonsense. It's a beginners' group, so the pace should be slow." Lorraine pointed to the listing in her amenities brochure.

Will leaned toward Lola. "If you'd like to skip the hike, I'd be happy to stay and keep you company."

"Would you?" she breathed.

"We can sit in the shade and enjoy an iced tea."

"Nonsense." Lorraine glared at Will. "Lola isn't spending her time like a bump on a log. I'll make certain the pace is slow enough for you, dear."

"If you're sure…?"

"Positive."

Will patted Lola's hand. "You know, I think I'll go on that hike, too. It sounds like fun."

Lorraine muttered something under her breath that sounded like "gold digger," but Kat thought she might have misunderstood. Will was such a nice guy.

Maybe she could learn to be attracted to a nice guy like him? After all, there wasn't some written rule that she had to have an instant chemical attraction to a man. Love at first sight certainly hadn't worked for her before. The only time she had seen it work was in the case of her best friend, Annie Marsh, and her husband, Drew Vincent.

"I was thinking of going on the hike," she interjected.

"Me, too," said a deep voice behind her.

Kat turned to see Tony merely inches away. Her pulse hammered in spite of her resolve.

"Why doesn't that surprise me?" She rolled her eyes.

"It shouldn't. I arrived here the same day you did and haven't had a chance to take the orientation hike yet. But, Sterling, I'd have thought you would have already taken it. You've been here a couple of days now, haven't you?"

"I have to confess I played golf my first two days. Met Kat on the shuttle because I was too lazy to lug my clubs back to my casita after I twisted my ankle."

"Say, I haven't golfed in a while, but we ought to play a round. Maybe scout up a foursome," Tony suggested. "The course here is supposed to be fairly challenging."

"Absolutely. Are you staying two weeks?"

Tony hesitated briefly, thinking of the mounting bill he was incurring for the Treadways. "Yep, I sure am."

"We'll definitely schedule something then. If you'll excuse me, I need to go change my clothes. I'll meet you all by the front desk."

"I need to get some sunblock." Kat took the opportunity to escape Tony and the pheremones he seemed to be giving off in waves. "I'll see you guys at the desk."

He stepped closer, his breath warm on her neck, raising goose bumps. "I bet you freckle and burn after five minutes in the sun."

Her mouth went dry as she tried to remember what they were discussing. Out of the corner of her eye, she noticed Lola and Lorraine exchange knowing glances.

"Um, yes...I burn." Kat glared at him as she turned to leave. She walked out with as much dignity as she could muster.

TONY WHISTLED under his breath as he approached the check-in area. It looked as if he was the first to arrive. It would give him an opportunity to locate the office before the others got there. He sure hoped he wouldn't need to access their files in an effort to find information.

It was a moot point, because Sterling—in khaki pants and a white golf shirt—arrived only moments later. A floppy canvas sun hat hung between his shoulder blades, suspended by a cord around his neck.

"Nice hat."

"I burn easily, too. Probably not a problem for you." His face was open and friendly, making Tony wonder if he'd imagined the slur on his Hispanic heritage. This guy was slick.

"Every once in a while." Tony shrugged, stepping over to pull a brochure from a nearby rack. Turning back to Will, he asked, "So where are you from?"

"Here and there. Most recently, Chicago."

Where he'd inherited a lovely condo from Eunice Treadway.

"Oh, you have family there?"

"No, I'm a widower."

It was all Tony could do not to laugh. Poor bereaved man. Yeah, right. He'd left Eunice the moment he'd drained her bank accounts. It had been sheer dumb luck that she hadn't changed her will after Sterling left, and he'd inherited the condo.

But Tony knew he should make some sort of appropriate response. "I'm sorry."

Will nodded. "How about you? Where are you from?"

"Texas."

"What brought you to Arizona?"

"I'd heard great things about this resort and I was way overdue for a vacation."

Sterling smiled as he gazed past Tony. "There you are."

Lola and Lorraine arrived, followed by the newlyweds.

Tony raised an eyebrow. He hadn't expected to see Troy and Angie for the remainder of their stay.

Four other men joined them, and then Linda's daughter, Brooke, arrived, clipboard in hand.

She called off names from the sign-up sheet, handing out chilled water bottles as she went.

The four men were executives from Transglobal Insurance, and had arrived a day early for a conference.

"I see you all have appropriate attire, comfortable shoes." Brooke was all business, impressive for someone not yet out of college. "It's important to stay hydrated, and sunblock is highly recommended."

Kat joined the group. Her cheeks were flushed and she was slightly out of breath. "Sorry I'm late."

"No problem." Brooke handed her a water bottle. "I was just advising about the importance of sunblock and staying hydrated. Sometimes the heat creeps up on us."

Kat nodded.

"Let's go."

As they filed out the double doors, Tony managed to stick close to Sterling and Lola.

Lorraine seemed intent on staying close, too.

If Will minded her constant presence, he was too smart to show it. He smiled broadly at both women. "It's a wonderful day for a hike."

"Wonderful," Lola echoed.

Will touched her arm. "I'm glad you decided to risk

it. It would have been a shame for you to have missed this."

"I'm still afraid I'll slow everyone down."

"Not a problem. I'll be here for you the whole way. If it gets too tough, you and I can always return to the resort and find a nice cool spot on the patio."

"Thank you. You're such a nice boy." Lola tucked her arm in his.

Tony felt a pang of sympathy for Lola. She was obviously a lonely woman who wanted attention. Attention Will was more than happy to provide.

Tony only hoped he could find solid evidence or leads before Lola got hurt. It was hard watching her fall under the man's spell and not be able to warn her.

Slowing his pace, he fell back, deep in thought. At some point Kat must have passed him, he suddenly realized, when the swing of her hips caught his attention.

Brooke's voice drifted back to him. "And on your left, in the distance, you might see petroglyphs carved into the cliff face, said to be left by the Yavapai Indians…."

Tony studied the cliffs and was just able to make out figures carved into the rock. "Amazing that they've been here for thousands of years, undisturbed by man."

"Amazing," Kat breathed, craning her neck and shielding her eyes with her hand. "In the city, it's easy to forget that Native Americans inhabited so much of Arizona."

"You grew up in Arizona?" Tony asked.

"I've lived in Tempe since I was a kid. It's a suburb of Phoenix."

"You're a city girl through and through?"

"Yes, and proud of it."

Brooke's voice became fainter.

"We'd better catch up." He grabbed Kat's hand and they started to jog. The incline was modest, the sun warm on his head. It was turning into a great day.

As soon as they met up with Sterling and Lola, the stragglers, Kat shook off his hand.

"Are you okay, Lola?" Tony asked.

"I'm…not…sure," the older woman puffed.

Will stopped. "Maybe we should go back."

"I'm just…a bit…light-headed."

Kat went to her side. "There's a boulder over there under the tree. Why don't you sit in the shade and catch your breath? Water will probably help."

"Okay."

She led the woman to the boulder. "Almost there… that's it…you're doing great."

Then Tony's Ranger training took over. "We need to get you cooled down. Where's your water?"

Will handed him the bottle.

Twisting off the cap, Tony pressed it into her trembling hand, guiding her wrist while she raised the bottle to her lips.

"Give me your bandanna, Kat."

She took it from her pocket, quickly handing it over. For once, she didn't argue. Her feistiness had been replaced by a worried frown.

He opened his own water container and poured some of the contents over the blue scarf. Folding it in thirds lengthwise, he placed it around Lola's neck and loosely tied it in the front. "That'll cool you off faster."

"Thank you." Her voice was barely a whisper.

They waited as she sipped her water. Several minutes later, she sighed. "I think I'm feeling better."

"You just got overheated." Will's tone held a note of authority.

"I can carry you piggyback to the resort," Tony said.

"I'm fine. It's probably just my blood pressure medication."

"You'll still want to seek medical attention, just to make sure." He wouldn't let her minimize the risk.

"I don't want to go to the doctor," she whined.

"There's no need to see the doctor if you don't want to, Lola." Will brushed a wisp of silver hair from her face. "He'll only send you to the emergency room, anyway, and that will ruin your trip. I'll take you back to your room."

Tony could have shaken the con man. He was obviously telling her what she wanted to hear, at the expense of caution. "I really think she should—"

"Does that sound okay to you, Lola?" Sterling interrupted, his face a mask of concern.

The hair at the back of Tony's neck prickled as the woman gazed up at Sterling and pressed her hand in his.

"Whatever you think, Will."

CHAPTER SEVEN

KAT WAS IMPRESSED WITH Will's selflessness. There was no way Zach would have even thought twice about an older woman's condition. Tony had been concerned, but now he seemed preoccupied.

A welcome breeze kicked up, along with ash tree leaves and dust. There wasn't a cloud in the sky, the May sun a bright yellow ball against the deep blue. The afternoon warmth combined with exercise would make the day seem like summer to those unaccustomed to the heat.

"I'll go with Lola," Kat offered.

Will shook his head, chuckling. "It's not like I'll miss the exercise—I'm the guy who rides the shuttle from the golf course. Let me have my dignity, will you?"

She couldn't help but smile as he laughed at himself.

She felt a sense of déjà vu when she said, "We'll let the others know. Is Lorraine just up ahead?"

Lola nodded. "She didn't…know…I fell behind."

"Could you tell her we went back? I don't want her out of sorts with me." Will winked, cupping Lola's elbow as he guided her to the trail.

"We'd better pick up the pace so the others don't worry." Tony cocked an eyebrow, as if assessing whether Kat were up to the exercise and heat.

Her sense of competition kicked in.

"Think you can keep up with me?" she challenged.

"Absolutely."

Kat took off at a near jog, no big deal until the trail inclined more steeply.

"Must be the altitude," she muttered under her breath.

Tony snorted. It was the only noise he made as he followed her, seemingly without effort. No labored breathing, no dropping behind.

When she glanced over her shoulder, she was dismayed to see he was a few steps behind her and wasn't even breaking a sweat.

Kat felt perspiration trickle between her shoulder blades. Tendrils of hair escaped her ponytail, curling damply against her cheeks.

Thank goodness her swim sessions at the Y kept her in shape, because number crunching sixty hours a week led to cellulite and high blood pressure. Or so some of the slightly older CPAs moaned.

Kat focused on putting one step in front of the other. Finally, they rounded a curve and saw the group ahead, waiting for them beneath a stand of trees.

"Not bad for a rookie." Tony swatted her behind as he passed her, sprinting for the group.

"Show-off," she grumbled, trying not to be distracted by his nice, tight rear end.

Bending over when they joined the others, she tried to catch her breath.

"You okay?" he asked.

"Fine."

Tony grinned. Then he turned to Lorraine. "Lola wasn't feeling well, so she and Will returned to the resort."

Lorraine swore under her breath. "Is she okay?"

Kat straightened, glancing at the older woman. She seemed more than concerned; she seemed angry. "We think she got a little overheated, but should be fine."

"Why is that man always hanging around my sister? It's not right and I don't like it."

Uh-oh. A case of sibling rivalry? Maybe she was afraid her sister would desert her. Kat had heard twins were often friends as well as siblings.

One look at Tony told her he was concerned, as well. "It is…unusual," he agreed.

"He's just being nice," Kat said in Will's defense.

"I wish I could be as trusting as you, but my father coddled Lola…protected her from experiencing harsh reality. And it seems as if her naiveté has grown worse in recent years. She's too trusting and some people take advantage of that."

Nodding, Kat thought she understood the situation better. "I'm sure she appreciates you looking out for her. I'd do the same for my sister if we were as close as you two. But I'm sure there's nothing to worry about."

Tony stepped closer to Kat, reaching to remove a twig from her hair. He focused his gaze on her mouth, and his voice was a warm caress as he said, "We could always return early. I'll race you. Winner buys drinks."

Her pulse pounded, but warning bells went off in her head. There was something not quite right about the way he suddenly seemed to have the hots for her. But she could hardly rely on her own instincts where men were concerned.

One thing was for sure—Tony confused her. She wished her hormones would stop clamoring for her to take him to bed.

"Well?" His voice was low, loaded with promise. He looked sexy standing there, damp, all male and… interested.

She glanced away from the heat in his gaze, determined not to surrender to his influence.

Troy and Angie were making out by a cypress tree a few feet away, oblivious to their surroundings. They were starting to get on Kat's nerves with their palpable lust. It certainly didn't help her keep calm, cool and collected.

One of the insurance executives said his group was ready to hit the bar.

Brooke sighed. "We might as well wrap this up for today. Nobody seems especially interested and I need to go check on Lola."

Tony nudged Kat with his shoulder.

Tightening her ponytail, she narrowed her eyes. "No bets are necessary. I predict I'll kick your butt."

With that, she took off running. Kat could hear footfalls behind her, but figured Tony had burned himself out with his show of speed earlier.

Sure enough, he lagged steadily behind.

Glancing over her shoulder, she confirmed that he was too far back to catch her.

The thrill of victory pounded through her blood.

THE LAYOUT OF Lola's suite was similar to his; a couch, two upholstered chairs and a coffee table delineated a sitting area ten feet from the doorway to the bedroom. A wet bar took up one corner near the door. And in the bedroom, instead of a king-size bed like his, there were two queens.

Will eased down on Lola's bed, taking her hand in his. "Are you feeling any better?"

"Yes, much." She smiled at him, stroking his hand as if he were a pet. "Thank you for taking care of me."

"It's my pleasure." He leaned close, tracing her dear, wrinkled cheek with his fingers.

"If only I were forty years younger…"

He smiled. The thrill never disappointed. "You're perfect just the way you are. Why would you want to be any different?"

She glanced away shyly.

He gently grasped her chin and tipped her face to look at him.

"I…wonder…if someone as young and handsome as you would be…interested…in someone like me?"

Ah, it was so easy. That told him he was doing the right thing. That he was meant to give back in just this way. He loved his vocation. And he loved the lifestyle it provided.

He leaned nearer, gazing at her puckered mouth. Pausing there, he let the suspense build.

After a moment, he shifted and lightly pressed his lips to hers, just a whisper of a touch.

He heard the beep of a key card milliseconds before the handle turned and the door opened.

He managed to pull back in the nick of time.

"Lorraine," they both exclaimed.

Will jumped to his feet, running his hand through his hair. "I'm glad you're here," he lied. "I think Lola only got overheated, but it's always best to be careful. She seems much better now."

"Yes." There was a bite to Lorraine's tone. "It *is* wise to be careful. That's why I have to wonder why you spend so much time with my sister."

Jealous old bat.

Will widened his eyes.

"Lorraine, don't be sharp with Will. He's been such a dear to help me." Lola's expression was slightly dreamy as she gazed at him.

Lorraine pushed past him and sat next to her sister on the bed, grasping her hand. "I know you're enjoying the attention. But it seems to me this particular man is after our money." She stared at him, daring him to deny it.

"You're wrong. Will isn't after my money." Lola raised her chin. "Are you?"

"Absolutely not...! I'm sorry, the last thing I wanted to do was upset you or your sister."

He managed a wounded expression, thinking of all the times people had wronged him, when all he'd wanted to do was help. Doctors were paid for their services, as were teachers and attorneys. It only stood to reason that he should receive some sort of remuneration.

"You've hurt his feelings, Lorraine. Apologize immediately." Lola's voice quavered. It came out as more of a plea than a demand.

Lorraine rose and strode over to him.

He resisted the urge to step backward, his natural response to her strong personality.

"Mr. Sterling, I'm very sorry if I've misjudged you. But I should advise you that Lola's money is tied up in an airtight trust. She agreed to let me make her financial decisions years ago when our father passed. With the exception of a small stipend."

Damn.

Will's heart sank. He hadn't counted on that. Suddenly, Lola appeared less in need of his help than he'd originally thought. And much as he liked her, he couldn't afford to spend more time on her if he couldn't recoup his expenses.

His bank balance was perilously low after he'd paid

for his stay at Phoenix Rising. His source at the travel agency had told him the Nash sisters would be here and they were loaded. That's all the encouragement he had needed. He absolutely had to earn some money while he was here.

"Will, are you all right?" Lola asked, a worried frown creasing her brow.

"Yes, I'm sorry. I was…shocked by Lorraine's accusations. I really have only the best intentions."

"You're…my friend. My sister, I'm sure will come around. Right, Lorraine?"

Lorraine crossed her arms. "If he's after your money it should become readily apparent now that he knows he'll never get his hands on it. I'm guessing he drops you immediately."

Great, just great. He had to search out a new…friend and benefactor. But he'd have to be careful. The last thing he needed was Lorraine kicking up a fuss.

Smiling reassuringly at Lola, he went to the side of the bed opposite Lorraine and leaned down to plant a tender kiss on Lola's forehead. "Your sister will soon realize I genuinely care for you. Now, you rest, and I'll call later to check on you."

TONY WAS GENERALLY in the zone when he jogged on the treadmill, but the next morning he was distracted by Sterling coming in and studying the corkboard.

What was the guy up to? Lorraine had told him she expected Will to drop Lola like a hot potato now that he knew her funds weren't easily accessible. But the con man had continued to be attentive to her last evening at dinner. Lorraine had watched him like a hawk.

Tony figured the man was simply biding his time. Patience was one of the key traits for a criminal like him. But Sterling had to be racking up a large tab, too.

Out of the corner of his eye, Tony noticed Will writing something on several sheets of paper attached to the board. Then he turned and walked out whistling.

Tony waited a few minutes, then shut down the treadmill and threw a towel around his neck. He sauntered to the board. Brooke was in the office doing paperwork, and he was the only guest using the gym this early.

It appeared Sterling had signed up to be Kat's doubles partner for tennis at nine this morning. And also joined a beginner's golf clinic tomorrow morning.

Sighing, Tony saw no other choice. This was the move he'd been anticipating. He had to keep an eye on this guy, even if tennis wasn't his game.

Fortunately, Tony was publicly pursuing Kat, so it wouldn't seem odd for him to join in. He scrawled his name as a partner for a Jennifer Randolph, playing opposite Kat Monroe and Will Sterling.

Brooke came out of the office. "I'm glad to see you're getting involved. I think you'll enjoy your stay more that way." She lowered her voice even though they were the only ones there. "And it gets Mom off my case. She seems to have great faith in my persuasive abilities."

"Yeah, moms…what can you do?" Tony muttered. What the hell was he getting himself into, playing tennis? Quite possibly, he was about to make a total ass of himself.

CHAPTER EIGHT

KAT EYED THE LEGGY BLONDE on the other side of the net. She was tossing her hair over her shoulder and laughing up at Tony; her short white tennis skirt and yellow halter top made Kat feel downright dumpy.

Glancing down at her cargo shorts and oversize tie-dye T, Kat sighed. Maybe a trip to the pro shop was in order? Somehow she doubted they would have anything her style in court attire.

Will walked over to her, handsome in his tennis whites. "I'm glad we're partners. We haven't had much chance to get to know each other."

His smile and the gleam of appreciation in his eye assuaged her wounded ego. Was he flirting with her?

"You may not be so thankful after you see me serve." She was going for perky, but came off sounding insecure.

Wonderful. Give her a jerk and she could bat her eyelashes and quip with the best of them. But with a quality guy, she might as well be a veteran wallflower.

"No problem. I can carry us."

Kat's competitive streak begged to differ. Maybe she hadn't played tennis since high school, but she could

make up for it with passion and determination. She
wanted his adoration, not his pity. "Let's hope that won't
be necessary."

He stepped close and cupped her elbow. "Sometimes
it's okay to let someone else carry the load. I just want
you to have fun, and not worry I'll throw a fit if we
lose."

"I wasn't…" Kat couldn't complete the sentence. He
was wrong. She wanted to win for herself, not because
she thought he couldn't handle losing. Or did she?

Forcing a smile, she said, "Okay. Good to know. A
lot of men can't stand to lose."

"I'm not a lot of men, Kat."

And she believed him. It was a new experience for her
to have a man more concerned about her than himself.
Imagine how that could translate in the bedroom?

Her temperature rose.

"That's sweet, Will." She glanced at their opponents;
Tony and the blonde, Jennifer, seemed to be deep in
discussion. Either plotting strategy or planning to go
back to her room for crazy hot sex.

Kat shielded her eyes from the sun and smiled up
into Will's face. He was beginning to seem pretty sexy.
"I wanted to tell you how impressed I've been with the
way you look after Lola. Not many men would do that,
either. I mean, the way you made sure to bring her back
one of her favorites when you went to the buffet table
this morning."

He shrugged, but seemed pleased. "She's great. It
takes so little to make her happy, so why not do a few

nice things for her? I feel bad that I haven't had time to get to know you better, though." He brushed a strand of hair from Kat's temple, his voice lowering. "But I intend to change that."

Finally.

Kat felt vindicated. She, Kat Monroe, could attract a nice, normal guy.

She managed to keep from gushing in her excitement. Instead, her response was simple, delivered with what she hoped was the right amount of enthusiasm. "I'd like that, Will."

"Hey, you two, are we going to play tennis or what?" Tony's tone sounded clipped.

"Anytime you're ready," Will called.

Kat's team won the coin toss and served first. Will's form was graceful, yet lightning fast.

The blonde returned his serve and the volley was on.

Kat soon recalled the nuances of the game and was able to hold her own.

Tony, however, attacked the ball as if every volley were a life and death battle. It was an approach that did not bode well for team spirit, and reminded Kat that Zach had always had to win, too.

But Jennifer didn't seem to care. She flirted outrageously, practically throwing herself at the man.

Kat was distracted when the two conferred privately. Tony tossed his head back and laughed at something the blonde said. Sun glinted off of his black hair, silver gleaming at his temples. He didn't touch Jennifer or

make obvious advances, but he certainly wasn't dis-
couraging her, either.

Shaking off her irritation at his fickle nature, Kat
told herself he was not relationship material and his
short attention span only proved it.

Jennifer seemed captivated by his muscular build,
taking every opportunity to touch his arm, his hand,
his shoulder.

The woman got on Kat's nerves.

"Don't worry, we can take them." Will winked at
her.

Somehow she wasn't so sure.

"We're waiting," Kat called.

Jennifer didn't seem to notice Kat's tone. She strutted
to the service line, her skirt moving with the exagger-
ated sway of her hips.

Kat could feel sweat bead her upper lip. She hated
to lose.

She and Will took their positions.

The woman reached for the sky with her racket as
she tossed the ball in the air. The yellow halter top
stretched taut across her breasts, propped up like ripe
melons against the low vee.

Kat figured Tony was getting an eyeful.

It was a competent serve, but not spectacular. Kat
was easily able to return it with a forehand stroke to
Tony. She and Will fell into an easy partnership of give
and take.

Tony, however, continued to be a ball hog. Kat drew
him out of position, so Jennifer had to run to protect the

back line. Kat took a vicious satisfaction in running her all over the court.

Tony saw what she was doing and settled into a form of teamwork. He honed his placement and soon became lethal. Jennifer got in a couple of lucky shots, too.

But Will was at home on the court and worked together with Kat to win, two games to one. At the end, they raised their hands and connected in a high five.

"We make a great team." His gaze lingered on her face.

"We certainly do."

She could have sworn he was going to ask her out, but the spell was broken when Tony and Jennifer came around the net to congratulate them.

"Not bad, Sterling. I can tell you know your way around the courts." Tony slapped Will on the back, knocking him forward half a step.

"Thank you. And you did well, too, though I'm guessing tennis isn't your game."

"Nope. I prefer my confrontations to be more direct," Tony said, whatever that was supposed to mean.

Jennifer muttered the requisite, "Good game," but only had eyes for Tony.

And Kat could see why. Sweat stained the neck of his gray T-shirt, formed to the planes of his chest. His biceps had flexed nicely with each shot. And she was annoyed to notice the man had legs to die for: strong, muscular and masculine. Why, oh why, did he have to have the goods to back up his arrogance? He would be so much easier to dismiss if he had a paunch and scrawny calves.

Shaking her head, Kat turned to Will, who looked as if he'd just stepped out of a Ralph Lauren ad. His blond hair gleamed in the sun. He wasn't even perspiring. And he focused totally on her, as if unaware that Jennifer was drop-dead gorgeous. He made Kat feel special.

His congratulatory hug stirred something inside her as the spicy scent of his no doubt expensive aftershave washed over her. Closing her eyes, she enjoyed the way she fitted into his arms, and how delicate he made her feel.

"Tony, would you mind walking me back to my casita?" Jennifer asked, practically batting her big, brown eyes. "I thought I saw…a coyote lurking in the brush and I'm…nervous. I've heard they can attack humans."

Kat couldn't help but snort. "Coyotes are nocturnal and shy."

"Maybe it was rabid." She tilted her head, fixing her bedroom eyes on Tony.

He took her arm. "Of course I'll walk you back. Which casita is yours?"

"Number two."

"That's right on our way. Sterling, Kat, you coming? We don't want to miss lunch."

"Sure," Kat said. "Will?"

"I need to stop off at my place to clean up first. I'm supposed to meet Lola and Lorraine in the dining room."

Kat smiled up at him. "You played great today. I'm glad you were my partner."

He linked his fingers with hers as they turned to follow Tony and the blonde. "Lola's a sweetheart, but…I won't have a chance to learn more about you." He rubbed the back of her hand with his thumb. The familiarity was soothing.

Kat could almost feel her world righting itself after the desolation of her breakup with Zach. There was something about Will that made her feel…whole.

"I'd like to learn more about you, too." She squeezed his hand. "Much more."

His smile was wide, as if she'd just given him the greatest gift. "Shall I save you a seat? It won't be as… intimate as I would like, but…" He shrugged. "Better yet, let's walk over together."

He was definitely attracted to her. That realization sent tingles of awareness through her.

Kat's heart skipped a beat. It was more than she had hoped for when she came to Phoenix Rising. Still, she'd packed a leopard-print camisole and matching thong as an affirmation of sorts. And it appeared she might get to wear them for Will before her vacation was over.

"I'd *love* to join you for lunch."

TONY GUIDED JENNIFER to the table next to Lorraine and Lola's after overhearing Will invite Kat to join them.

"Hello, Lola, Lorraine."

"Hello, Tony." Lorraine waved. Lola listlessly pushed her food around on her plate with a fork.

"Mind if we sit with you?"

"Please do."

"Jennifer?" Tony held out a chair for her.

She frowned, but recovered quickly, sinking into it gracefully.

As he made the introductions, Lola kept glancing toward the entrance.

Finally, she asked, "Did you see Will when you came in? He's usually right on time."

"We played him in doubles tennis this morning and he said something about taking a shower before lunch. Don't worry, I'm sure he'll be along shortly."

"Unless Lorraine offended him with all her talk about him being a gold digger."

"I'm sure he realizes your sister is only looking out for your best interests."

"I'm seventy-three, plenty old enough to look out for myself. And I want Will..." she glanced sideways at her sister "...to be my friend."

"If you hadn't always been daydreaming and making foolish choices, nobody would question your independence," Lorraine muttered. "As it is, I'm trying to help you."

"Will isn't after my money. He was very attentive at breakfast even after you told him about the trust."

"Maybe he's smarter than I gave him credit for and doesn't want to look obvious."

Tony followed the sibling bickering with interest.

Maybe Lorraine was right and Sterling had more tricks up his sleeve. If so, Tony intended to be there to catch him.

Glancing up, Tony saw the subject of their discussion arriving with Kat. He didn't like the proprietary way the man guided her to their table. But it was none of his business what she did.

Will pulled out Kat's chair for her, before turning to Lola. "You're looking well. Did you and Lorraine enjoy your spa treatments?"

Lola's face lit with pleasure. "It was lovely. Though I missed you."

"And I missed you, too." He patted her on the shoulder, while his gaze roamed over Kat, who had changed into a Hawaiian print sarong that left one pale shoulder bare. Bare except for a sprinkling of tiny freckles.

Freckles that prompted Tony to wonder where else she might have them. The thought shocked him because it was definitely not within the scope of his investigation. He didn't usually forget the boundaries when he was working.

Jennifer leaned in and whispered, "He's quite the charmer."

"Who?"

"Will."

Shaking his head, Tony realized he'd momentarily forgotten Jennifer while focusing on Kat's silky shoulder.

He shrugged. "I guess. If you like that type."

Jennifer glanced sideways at him. "I don't. I prefer my men more rugged and…dangerous."

He lifted his glass, taking a swig of iced tea. He'd never thought of himself as dangerous, though Corrine had pointed out he was hardly the homebody type. Was that what she'd meant? At the time, he'd thought it was a backhanded swipe at the number of hours he worked. His ex-wife had kept so much bottled up inside, he'd never known what was going on with her until it was too late. He still wasn't completely sure when she'd become so unhappy. All she would say was that they'd "grown apart over time." What the hell did *that* mean?

Jennifer gazed at him expectantly.

Wiping his mouth with his napkin, he chose a safe topic. "How long have you been at the resort?"

"A week. We…I mean I…leave tomorrow. But I could be persuaded to stay longer…?"

He allowed her unspoken question to trail off into oblivion, uneasy at her accidental use of the plural. He suspected many men would overlook the slip. But he wasn't the average guy. He missed the passion, the closeness of being with a woman who knew the best and worst about him and loved him anyway. At least that's how it had been with Corrine in the early years, when they couldn't keep their hands off of each other. And now he wouldn't settle for less. Nor would he help break someone else's wedding vows.

Instead, he reminded himself of his purpose. "So Will, how long did you say you're staying?"

"Two weeks, maybe longer. I don't have another consulting assignment for three weeks."

"You must tell me more about your work as a life coach." Lola grasped Will's hand. "There are some… issues…I could use help with. I'm sure the trust administrator would have no objection to me hiring you."

"He damn well better." Lorraine squared her shoulders. "And if he doesn't, I'll certainly set him straight."

"Now, Lorraine—"

"Don't 'now, Lorraine' me. Someone's got to have sense around here. And it's obviously not you."

Lola's lower lip trembled. "You just don't want me to have fun."

"I've spent most of my life saving you from one bad decision or another. This is no different."

Will stood slowly, his shoulders stiff. "Lola, I'm sorry. I can't stand by while Lorraine slanders me."

"I'm sure Will doesn't mean any harm, Lorraine," Tony lied, though it pained him to say it.

"Thank you. I only want to help. But I seem to be making things harder on you, Lola." He turned to Kat. "Under the circumstances, I think it would be best if we found another table."

Kat glanced at Lorraine, then back at Will. "Surely this is all a misunderstanding."

"Lorraine…" Lola's voice rose. "Apologize immediately."

Jennifer shifted nervously. Obviously she didn't do well with conflict.

Tony, on the other hand, could appreciate what a good ally Lola had in Lorraine. If Eunice Treadway had had a sister like her, she would still be alive, watching her two granddaughters grow into young women. He didn't dare let his thoughts show, though.

"Maybe we should move, too," Jennifer whispered.

"Lorraine, you've gone too far this time. Apologize or else I'll...I'll—"

"You'll what? Go off on some other harebrained scheme? Then come crying to me when it blows up in your face?" Lorraine stood, her eyes flashing. "Kat, you're welcome to stay. But, Will, it would be best if you went far, far away. Because I have the power to make you sorry if you don't. Very sorry."

Sterling's face flushed as he threw down his napkin and gathered his plate.

His gaze was stony as he turned to Kat. "Well?"

Kat bit her lip.

CHAPTER NINE

KAT FELT HER CHEEKS flush with embarrassment for Will. But she couldn't hold it against Lorraine, who was obviously accustomed to looking out for her sister.

All the while, she was acutely aware of Tony watching her, as if this was some test of *her* character. Probably her imagination, because the man obviously didn't care what she did. Otherwise, he wouldn't allow Jennifer to trail her fingers possessively down his forearm.

Kat rose slowly. It seemed as if everyone stared at her as she did.

"I don't want you eating all by yourself, Will." Turning to the sisters, she said, "I'm sorry."

What she was apologizing for, she had no idea.

Kat reluctantly followed Will to a vacant table at the far side of the room. It was all she could do not to glance over her shoulder at the people who were rapidly becoming almost like family to her. It went against every molecule in her being to walk away.

When her parents had divorced, it seemed as if Kat lost her mother and sister, because Kat had stayed with her father. They'd become two separate, smaller family units. That blow had been more horrible than she could have ever imagined, almost like a death.

Maybe that's why she had such a hard time when people left her. Why she clung to men even when they were no good for her. Heck, why she chose them in the first place. Because anything was better than being alone.

"No need to look so sad." Will's spine was taut as he sat, shaking out a new cloth napkin.

"Lorraine doesn't understand," Kat said softly once she took her seat.

"Some people aren't happy unless everyone around them is miserable."

"I haven't had that impression of Lorraine at all. If anything, I admire her zest for life."

He turned, frowning.

Kat quickly tried to smooth his ruffled feathers. "I'm sure she didn't mean to sound...harsh. Let's not let it spoil our lunch." Kat leaned forward and held his gaze in what she hoped was an alluring manner, trying to distract him. It was a look that Zach had said no man could resist. And yet *he* had. Many times, toward the end. "It'll be kind of nice to have you all to myself."

Will clasped her hand. "Absolutely. Thank you for pointing out the silver lining."

Squeezing his hand, she released it to place her napkin on her lap. "My father always said I had a knack for looking on the bright side."

"Are you close with your family?"

Kat bit into her club sandwich, chewing slowly,

reluctant to talk about such a sensitive topic. After swallowing, she said, "My mom and dad are divorced. I don't see my dad much since he remarried twelve years ago."

"How about your mother?"

"We talk frequently. She's...distracted right now. My sister is pregnant and due in two weeks with the first grandchild. Mom's staying with her until after the baby's born." Kat kept her voice light, refusing to confide how hard it was to see motherhood slipping away from her. Or how badly she wanted to feel a part of the tight little circle her mother and sister had become with her brother-in-law. Problem was, Kat had no idea how to begin breaking through decades of barriers.

LINDA STOPPED BY THEIR table. "There you two are. I'm signing people up for the Jasper tour this afternoon. You'll love it."

Kat hesitated. "I'd kind of wanted to sit poolside with a novel."

"We need at least six to commit and we have only two so far," Linda said, using every trick in the book to get them to agree. "If you've never seen Jasper before, you won't want to miss it. Lots of history and great little one-of-a-kind shops. And a few places to get a drink and have quiet conversation. There are even several spots said to be haunted."

"That clinches it for me. Come on, Kat. I'll go if you go." Will sat back and waited.

Slowly, she smiled. Experiencing new things was

what she'd wanted, wasn't it? And running into a ghost might be fun. "All right."

Linda jotted their names on her clipboard. "Great. See you at one-thirty at the front entrance."

"See you then." Kat turned to Will. "I guess I can't be this close to Jasper without seeing the famous brothels."

"And the very best part is we'll be together." His tone was loaded with meaning. His gaze lingered on her mouth, as if he was contemplating kissing her.

Something told her Will would be a great kisser. She shifted. The room had certainly gotten warmer.

"What are you thinking about?" He traced her bottom lip with his thumb. "You're sexy when you're pensive."

If he only knew. Pensive? Or pent-up?

She couldn't for the life of her imagine Zach using the first term. Or Tony for that matter.

Just thinking about the dark, confusing man made her breath catch. And that scared the living daylights out of her. This vacation was supposed to begin her transformation into a mature woman who could attract and love a nice guy, without being distracted by a man who would surely run away if he knew Scaredy-Kat, as her dad used to call her. The girl afraid of losing people.

Will, on the other hand, seemed to make allowances for foibles and imperfections.

"I'm thinking…I'm glad you're here," she confessed. "And glad we're going on the Jasper excursion." He was handsome, intelligent, charming and financially stable. What more could she want?

A tall, good-looking man with silver at his temples came to mind, but she quickly pushed the thought away. She touched Will's shoulder, as much to ground herself as to underscore her interest.

He rested his forearm lightly on the back of her chair. "I need to go make some phone calls first. I'll stop by your room to pick you up about one-fifteen?"

"That would be great. I'm looking forward to it."

His eyes gleamed as he surveyed her from head to toe. "I am, too. Believe me, I am, too."

IT WAS ALL TONY COULD DO to pry Jennifer from his side and return her to her room. Fortunately, her husband was due to arrive this afternoon, a husband she'd neglected to mention until Tony pressed her. After Tony had avoided her suggestion of adjourning to the privacy of his casita, she'd immediately lost interest in him.

He still respected marriage vows, even if she didn't. Shaking his head, he wondered if he was cut out for this single stuff. It certainly hadn't been his choice. If it had, he would still be a married Ranger.

Had Corrine cheated on him when he'd spent those long hours at work? Maybe it hadn't been a case of gradually growing apart, but instead being replaced in one of the most intimate areas of his marriage.

Tony discounted the possibility. He might have taken Corrine for granted, but he doubted he would have been too stupid to miss the signs of straying. He was a professional investigator, dammit.

Kat and Will strolled ahead of him, hand in hand, emphasizing how alone he was in a world of couples. The sight made his stomach lurch. It sure hadn't taken the con man long to set his sights on her after Lorraine had chased him off.

A shift that disturbed Tony more than it should have. The thought of Kat being taken in by Will was just as repugnant as an old woman being blindsided. Maybe because Tony sensed that on some level Kat was every bit as vulnerable.

He quickened his pace. "Hey, you two. Looks like we'll be together on the Jasper tour. Linda insisted that I go."

Kat dropped Sterling's hand. "Ah, yes, we were conscripted by her, too. There was no easy out."

"It should be…interesting." Tony looked forward to mixing business with pleasure while sightseeing. "Jasper was a wild place back in the day. A Western town, complete with miners and saloon girls."

"I'm beginning to sense a theme here. You guys are just interested in the old bordello, aren't you?"

He grinned. "Nothing wrong with mixing a history lesson with beautiful women."

Will draped his arm over Kat's shoulders, marking his territory. It was enough to make Tony want to deck the guy.

Because he knew what Sterling really was beneath his good-guy veneer. And Tony couldn't stand to see that raw, vulnerable look in Kat's eyes when she realized Sterling had used her, made a fool of her. The same hurt he'd seen after he'd kissed her on the playground that first day.

Only this time it wouldn't be just a harmless kiss with a relative stranger. It would mean the loss of everything she valued: her money, pride, self-respect, what little trust in men she still had.

And Tony wouldn't be able to do a damn thing to prevent it unless he could find hard evidence first.

"We're just helping Linda out," Sterling said. "Otherwise, we'd planned on lounging around the pool, slathering sunblock on each other."

Surprise flashed in Kat's eyes. So, this was news to her.

Tony reined in his antagonism. "Well, I'll see you two at the van later then."

He was glad the path to his place branched off, so Sterling wouldn't see he'd gotten to him. The mere thought of the man's filthy hands on Kat's body was enough to make Tony sick.

He stopped in the middle of the walkway. Somewhere along the line he'd begun to believe his own pretext. He had…feelings for Kat. The thought was as disturbing as it was unlikely. It meant his priorities had shifted. He was losing his professional detachment, one of his most valued tools both as a Ranger and a private investigator.

Swearing under his breath, he strode to his casita.

More than ever he needed to get evidence on Sterling, and soon. This had gotten personal.

Unlocking the door, he went to stare out the glass Arcadia door at the desert foothills beyond. But it wasn't the view that held his attention. It was the realization that there were no bars to wedge at the bottom of the frame for security. It would be simple to jimmy one of these doors off the track, an oversight he was surprised to see in a resort of this caliber. The idea of pitching improved security to Linda and Garth for the whole facility warred with the temptation of how easily he could break into Sterling's room. An option Tony hadn't had in the Rangers. And once inside, he might luck out and find evidence that Sterling had defrauded Treadway and probably others.

The hair on the back of his neck prickled. Weren't fewer rules and less red tape supposed to be the benefits of private investigation? The Treadways certainly wouldn't care where he found the key to putting Will behind bars.

Tony turned from the expanse of glass. Following procedure had been ingrained for too long. He wouldn't risk a felony by breaking and entering. But time was running out. If he didn't find out anything from Sterling soon, he would sacrifice rules and procedures before he sacrificed Kat.

He refused to contemplate why he was willing to bend the rules for her and no one else.

Tony hoped it wouldn't be necessary to find out.

Booting up his computer, he checked his e-mail and

returned a few calls on his cell. One client wanted to vent about his wife's affair, and Tony listened patiently for the first five minutes. Sometimes his role seemed to be as much therapist as private investigator. What he wouldn't give to hand this part off to an associate…. No victims' services here, though.

When Tony had had enough of the hand-holding, he told the guy he had another call and would touch base with him next week, hoping like hell his client's divorce attorney didn't need any more documentation.

As it was, Tony was nearly late to meet with the Jasper group. Linda had apparently rounded up enough folks to fill two vans. Tony could have ridden in the second one, but he chose to go with Sterling, and ride shotgun with Garth. Tony grinned when he observed the seat assignments, which must have taken NATO to negotiate. In the back, the newlyweds, Troy and Angie, cuddled in a corner. Will sat as far to the left as he possibly could, leaning against the panel. Kat, Lola and Lorraine shared the middle seat.

Excellent. Will had been separated from Kat and didn't have the option of making out the whole way to Jasper.

Tony fell into a comfortable conversation with Garth for a few minutes, then listened to the voices behind him. Much to his satisfaction, Will quickly abandoned efforts to chat up Kat. And she seemed content to listen to the twins.

They made good time, and it seemed only minutes

later that Garth squeezed the van into a parallel parking space along Main Street.

"Nice job," Tony commented.

"Thanks. Parking is at a premium here." He turned in his seat to address the other passengers. "Watch your step getting out. Jasper is built on the side of a hill. Some of the walkways are steep and uneven."

Tony got out and opened the sliding door, noticing the other van was parked three or four vehicles behind them. He extended his hand to Kat.

She eyed it as if it might bite, and hopped down without his assistance.

"Show-off," he said, just loudly enough for her to hear.

But she pretended she didn't. In fact, she ignored his existence entirely.

He chuckled. At least he always knew where he stood with her.

Reluctantly, Tony directed his attention to the twins.

"Take it slowly, Lola," he said. "I'll help."

She grasped his hand and he steadied her as she wobbled. "Thank you, dear."

"Lorraine?"

The old woman winked at him as he assisted her from the vehicle. Then pinched his rear end when his back was turned.

He grinned over his shoulder. "Watch it, lady. I might put you over my knee."

Her laughter floated back to him. "In your dreams, young man, in your dreams."

"You've got it from here, don't you, Sterling?" Tony asked, then didn't wait for an answer. Instead, he sauntered over to where Kat stood in the shade of an ash tree in the small front yard of a clapboard bed-and-breakfast.

She folded her arms when she saw him approach. But not before he noticed the way her gaze lingered appreciatively on his pecs and biceps. His ex-wife used to like the way his Dallas Cowboys T-shirt hugged his frame. Said the soft, worn fabric was darn near like being naked. He was glad he'd abandoned the baggy Hawaiian print shirts.

"Interested in what you see?" Tony asked Kat.

"Not particularly."

"Liar."

Her mouth twitched for a fraction of a second.

"Don't smile. I might think you like me," he goaded her.

"I don't like you and I don't dislike you. I'm like Switzerland—neutral."

He stepped closer. "Darlin', the only thing neutral about you is the khaki color of your shorts. The purple top and matching polish gives you away as a girlie girl. Oh, and the jeweled sandals, too."

"The color is fuchsia."

"Whatever it is, I like it." He reached over and tugged on her ponytail. The stubborn tilt to her chin was starting to grow on him, too.

He was about to tell her so when they heard a shout from the direction of the vans.

Spinning around, Tony saw Sterling lying prone on the ground, with the newlyweds standing over him, shouting for help.

CHAPTER TEN

KAT RUSHED TO WILL'S SIDE, but the young husband, Troy Birmingham, helped him to his feet.

"Are you all right?" she asked, as Will brushed dirt off the seat of his pants.

"I twisted my weak ankle, but I don't think it's too bad. I tripped over a loose cobble." He pointed toward the van, parked along a cobblestone street. His weight seemed to be fully on his left leg, with his right knee bent, and his toes touching to help him balance.

Kat stepped closer, careful to avoid the cobblestone. "Why don't you lean on me while you test your weight."

Will put his arm around her shoulders, tucking her close to his side. They fitted together so nicely. She breathed in the delicious scent of his cologne.

"Here, why don't you lean on me, Sterling. You might hurt Kat." Tony's gaze was intense.

Kat wrapped her arm around Will's waist. "He's fine. Really."

Shifting more of his weight onto her, he gingerly tested his right foot. Slowly, he eased back, smiling, as his hand crept to just below her breast. "Not too bad at all. I think I can get around on my own."

"Yeah, that's great." Tony clapped him on the shoulder again and drew him away from Kat. "I bet there's a family-practice doctor here in town who would be willing to look at that ankle."

Will glanced in her direction, mouthing, *"Thank you."*

"You ready to find that doctor?" Tony prodded. "We can ask Garth to recommend someone."

"I don't think that's necessary." Will turned to Kat. "Where would you like to go first? The haunted hotel or the shops along Copper Square?"

She opened the brochure they'd been given. Looking around, she noticed the old, clapboard hotel was up a steep hill, while the sidewalk sloped gently down to the winding streets below. Trees were few because of the rocky soil, according to the highlights she'd read. Copper had once been the lifeblood of the town.

"The map indicates Copper Square is one street over, at the bottom of the hill. Why don't we try that first?"

Lorraine shook her head. "I'm afraid Lola might not be able to make it back up the hill once we got down there. I think we'll find the little teahouse on Silver Butte Way. We'll meet you at the van later."

Lola opened her mouth to protest, but Garth threaded his left arm through hers. "Ladies, I have a confession to make." He offered his right arm to Lorraine. "I'm addicted to the scones they serve at the teahouse. Do you mind if I accompany you?"

"We'd be delighted." Lorraine accepted his arm.

Kat suspected Lorraine would agree to almost anything to keep Lola separated from Will. It was too bad, because Will was not that sort of guy. She admired the way he'd put his embarrassing fall behind him. It was nice to find a man who didn't resort to macho posturing.

"Are we agreed then?" she asked him. "Shopping first, then see how your ankle is doing?"

"You are so warm and caring, Kat. You should have been a nurse. Shopping it is."

Worrying her bottom lip, Kat told herself a really giving person would invite Tony to go with them, since he seemed to be odd man out. Yet she hesitated to include him. Mostly because he was bigger than life and comparisons with Will seemed inevitable and distracting.

But Will saved her from her dilemma. He draped his arm around her shoulder. "Don't let us keep you, Tony. We'll meet you at the van at five o'clock. See ya."

Glancing back, Kat was surprised to see a frown creasing Tony's brow, though he quickly hid his concern. Surely he wasn't worried about her?

"I'll tag along with you two. I'm always up for… shopping." His flat expression told her he'd rather have a bikini wax. "Besides, you might turn that ankle again and need help up the hill."

"I'll be fine."

"No problem. No problem at all."

With that, he managed to insinuate himself on Kat's other side, effectively making Will walk in the narrow street. She would've found Tony's persistence amusing, except she was supposed to be on a date with Will. It was too early to expect to be falling in love, but a severe case of lust would be more than welcome.

Lust. How long had it been since she'd felt the unmistakable undercurrent that made her want to be reckless again? Not since the early days of dating Zach—probably nearly three years.

What if she was no longer capable of lust? Her steps faltered.

Tony grasped her elbow, his voice like the warm, buttery smoothness of a hot toddy on a frigid evening as he said, "Careful, darlin'."

She blamed her slower-burning attraction to Will on Tony's persistent presence.

"I've got her." Will pulled her closer.

Kat missed the warmth of Tony's hand when he withdrew, but enjoyed the secure feeling of snuggling into Will.

This was crazy.

Why couldn't she shake her attraction to Tony? Her gut told her he was a dangerous man. Dangerous because he seemed to be able to see her as she was, flaws and all. It didn't take long for a man like that to tire of the real Kat. The stay-at-home-in-her-fuzzy-slippers Kat. The one with issues and an insidious lack of perfection.

Kat was done with men like that. Because they always left her feeling as if they'd stolen a piece of her soul. And some days, it felt as if she didn't have too many pieces left to give.

She raised her chin. "Doesn't it bother you being a fifth wheel?"

During a break in traffic, they carefully moved around a group of Asian tourists, into the narrow street.

Tony shrugged. "That depends on how you define fifth wheel. A spare sure can come in handy in a crisis. But no, it doesn't bother me at all. Which store are we going to try first?"

WILL WISHED TONY WOULD mind his own business. Will was having a hard enough time establishing a lasting rapport with Kat without this interference.

Maybe he'd been helping too many older women and no longer knew how to insinuate himself into the heart of a young, vital one.

He had to admit, the thought of Kat in bed was a good deal more attractive than the thought of Lola. Lola was wonderful, but he suspected it would have been difficult to work up sufficient enthusiasm to prove his love. Before he'd found his calling, Will had been under the mistaken impression that older women weren't interested in sex anymore. He couldn't have been more wrong. Usually a roll in the sheets was the very thing that would earn an older woman's undying affection.

Feeling Kat's warm, firm curves pressed against his

side, he wanted to laugh aloud. Once he'd worked his magic, her lottery nest egg would be perfect to tide him over until he could make a big score.

"What are you smiling about?" The breeze whipped a strand of hair into her eyes. She brushed it away.

Leaning in, he kissed her unlined cheek. Too bad about the faint sprinkling of freckles. But he wouldn't let that dampen his enjoyment of the chase. "I was thinking what a lucky man I am to have your company today. I'm glad you came with me."

"What a sweet thing to say."

Yes, it was. And it was only the beginning.

TONY PRETENDED HE DIDN'T notice Will planting a kiss on Kat's cheek. Pretended his blood pressure hadn't spiked.

Though less wrenching, it wasn't so different from how he'd felt sitting across the conference table from Corrine's attorney as the man blithely advised him how their marriage would be divided up—sixteen years of till-death-do-us-part symbolized in money and things. Tony had wanted to grab the guy by his expensive shirt collar and make him feel some of his pain.

Tony was disturbed that a woman could bring out those strong emotions in him after less than a week.

Think what she could do after sixteen years.

He watched Kat out of the corner of his eye. Was she buying Sterling's BS?

And what would Tony do if she was? Stand by and

watch, so he could catch Sterling committing a crime? His job, his case, demanded he do just that.

Still, he couldn't stop himself from hauling her toward a small shop and away from Will. "Look, an antique bookstore. Let's go inside."

Like the true parasite he was, Will held on tightly to her other arm.

Kat laughed, her cheeks flushing pink. "I didn't know you were such a devoted reader."

"There's a lot you don't know about me." Tony held the door for her, tempted to let it close on Sterling. But it wouldn't do to allow his dislike to become noticeable.

At least Will let go of her. For now.

Thank God Tony's cover enabled him to treat the other man as a competitor, and nobody would think it odd. It was perfect, as a matter of fact. Access to Sterling, but no need to hide his instincts to get into a pissing match when the guy tried to put the moves on Kat.

Tony suddenly felt freer than he had all day.

"What do you read?" he asked her.

She glanced sideways at him, but played along. "You're probably going to think this is weird, but I love political thrillers."

"Really?" He raised an eyebrow. "Clancy? Flynn?"

"Yes on both counts. Flynn is my favorite, though I'll read Clancy or Baldacci in a pinch."

"You're kidding."

"Why would I kid about something like that?"

"My ex-wife said the only people who read political thrillers are terrorists and retired law enforcement types."

"Well, she can add CPAs to the list."

Will pushed himself between them. "I'm fond of the classics myself."

Of course. Pretentious bastard.

"It looks like those are over there." Tony pointed toward the far wall about a hundred feet away, where books were stacked and shelved in every imaginable space.

"Kat, let's see if there are any first editions," Will suggested.

She smiled halfheartedly. "I'd really like to find a good thriller to read while I'm on vacation."

Shrugging, he said, "Suit yourself," and limped away.

Tony was already thumbing through a Stephen Coonts book. "I left this one on my nightstand at home. I could have kicked myself. I had only a couple of chapters left."

Kat came to stand next to him and he handed her a book. "Have you read this?"

Shaking her head, she opened it to scan the dust jacket.

A raised voice interfered with his enjoyment of watching her read. "Bill Powers, there should be a special place in hell for men like you."

An older, heavyset woman seemed to be directing her comment to Will.

He glanced up and his eyes widened.

"I'm sorry," he said slowly, "but you're mistaken. I'm not Bill...Powers?"

She stepped closer to him, poking him in the chest. "Where's my money?!"

"I've never seen you before in my life." He edged backward. "You're obviously confused."

"I'm not confused." But her voice held a trace of doubt.

"I have one of those faces.... People are always mistaking me for someone else. I'm sure that's what's happened."

"I—I could have sworn..."

"It's okay." Will smiled.

"You're sure you weren't in Kansas City five years ago?"

"Positive. Like I said, you've obviously confused me with someone who resembles me."

Doubt clouded her face.

The clearly embarrassed bookseller called to her from behind the counter. "Mrs. Deveraux, I'll phone up to the Four Winds if I get that first edition in."

"Yes...that's fine," the woman murmured. She stopped at the threshold as she was about to leave the store, and looked back at Will. Finally, she turned and walked out. Tony noted that she headed up the hill in the direction of the bed-and-breakfast hotels.

He decided maybe he should drive into town tomorrow and look up a certain Mrs. Deveraux.

CHAPTER ELEVEN

KAT CAUGHT WILL'S EYE across the store. He tapped his temple, rolling his eyes.

"That was odd." She placed the book back on a shelf.

"Like he said, maybe she was mistaken." Tony's casual tone belied the tension emanating from him.

"Must have been."

She tried to recapture her enjoyment of sharing books with, of all people, Tony. He was proving to have more dimensions than she'd imagined. A fact that was rapidly moving him from the dangerous category to the devastating. Dangerous meant she could eventually recover from the pain. She could only imagine how a devastating man might level her.

Clearing her throat, she asked, "Is there…a good series you can recommend?"

"Hmm? Oh, um, series… Yeah." He moved to the next shelf, where the books were filed alphabetically by author. Selecting one, he handed it to her. "This guy's new. If his first book is any indication, it's going to be a killer series. No pun intended."

"Thanks." Smiling in spite of herself, Kat knew she was in trouble.

His responding smile was wide, revealing the slight dimple. His gaze met hers and something profound shifted in her.

She sucked in a breath, her response instant and visceral. The small bookstore faded away, along with rational thought. It was as if his unselfconscious smile reached a place inside her that *knew* him. No matter how she fought it, it was absolutely right for her to be with him today. No, not just today. Always.

Kat tried to deny the unwelcome certainty that Tony could be important to her. She'd always feared that guys who had it all—brains, looks, a career—eventually would realize she wasn't enough. She might turn herself inside out, change herself to be whatever he wanted, and in the end, Tony would still leave her when someone better came along. At least the bad boys never left, because on some cellular level, they *needed* her. As a crutch, a trophy, a mommy or a paycheck, it didn't matter. She was indispensible. And that gave her the security she needed.

Kat blinked, the enormity of how she'd sold herself out over the years hitting her hard.

"What's wrong? You look like you've seen a ghost." Tony grasped her hand in both of his, warming her with his touch. "You're like ice. Maybe we should go out in the sun."

"Yes, you're probably right," she said, still feeling

out of sync with the rest of the world. She had enough presence of mind to remove her hand from his.

It wasn't until they were outside that she remembered three of them had gone into the store and only two had left. "What about Will?"

Tony's eyes glinted with mischief. "I don't suppose we could ditch him?"

Kat's survival instincts kicked in, telling her she had to distance herself from Tony, and do it quickly. "No, we can't. And I don't want to."

Liar.

She wanted nothing more than to leave Will behind and spend the rest of the afternoon with Tony. Maybe at one of those bed-and-breakfasts, naked, taking the afternoon and evening to explore each other beneath downy white comforters. Heck, why stop there? Maybe spend the rest of her vacation with Tony, in and out of bed.

No!

That's what the old Kat would have done. And promptly invited him to move in with her.

"I'll go get him."

She found Will behind a bank of shelves near the classics section. He was leaning his forehead against a shelf and his eyes were closed.

She touched his arm. "Are you okay?"

He opened his eyes and straightened. "I'm fine. My ankle is worse than I originally thought. I think I'd better return to the van."

"Of course. Do you want to lean on me?"

Shaking his head, he said, "Not quite the strong male image I wanted to project. I'm sorry, Kat, I was looking forward to sightseeing with you." He smoothed her hair away from her face. "Rain check?"

"Of course." She breathed a sigh of relief. Will was solid, familiar and nice in a way Tony wasn't.

Will cupped her cheek with his hand. "Would you have dinner with me tonight? In my room?"

Kat shifted. "I'm not sure if—"

"I'm not trying to seduce you." His mouth twisted as he gestured toward his ankle. "It would just be easier on my leg."

"Oh." Remorse hit her hard. "I—I didn't think about that."

But she *had* been thinking it was a prelude to seduction. Which might have been welcome at a different time or under different circumstances.

Different circumstances or different man?

Kat blushed.

Will lightly touched her hip. "I'm sorry if I made you uncomfortable. That's the last thing I wanted to do. I like you, Kat. I hope you know that." He held her gaze, rubbing her cheek with his thumb.

"I...like you, too."

"Good." Holding the back of her neck, he leaned in, his voice low. "I find you very attractive. But we'll take it at a pace you're comfortable with."

"Thank you." And yet Kat wondered. He'd gotten so touchy-feely even as he was saying he'd keep the pace slow. She pulled away. "We better go. Tony is waiting for us."

She headed toward the door. When she glanced over her shoulder, Will was limping slowly, his face taut with pain. Or was it something else?

TONY SIGHED IN RELIEF as the cab pulled away from the curb outside the bookstore. "Do you think his ankle really hurts that bad?"

"What a horrible thing to ask. But then again, I'm not always a great judge of character."

"Yeah, I noticed that."

"What's that supposed to mean?" Kat's blue-green eyes flashed. "Maybe that I shouldn't be here talking to you, when a perfectly nice guy wanted to buy me dinner?"

"Believe me, darlin', Sterling isn't all he seems. I'd bet my last dollar."

"Why?"

Tony crossed his arms, wishing he could give her a wake-up call, tell her what he knew about this "nice guy."

He was saved from answering right away when a couple he'd seen from the second van came out of the bookstore and stood next to them. They were deciding between the tea shop and the former bordello. They reached a compromise, but only because the husband agreed to have tea after touring the bordello. They headed toward the saloon.

Resuming their conversation, Tony said, "I just have a gut feeling about Sterling."

"Well, your gut is wrong. He's been nothing but a gentleman to me." Yet she glanced away. What wasn't she telling him?

He gently turned her face so he could look at her. "There's something bothering you. What?"

A family of four—a couple and two teenagers—jostled them as they made a beeline for the ice cream shop next door.

"Nothing." Kat sounded like a defiant two-year-old. "Okay, he invited me to dinner in his room…but only because it will be easier on his injured ankle."

Tony wanted to pull her close and kiss her until she forgot about any other man. Again, this wasn't a line he'd ever been tempted to cross on a case before, and he still didn't like what it said about his professionalism. "Any man who invites you to his room has seduction on his mind. Either that, or he's gay. Which is it with Will?"

"He said he would take…this…at a slower pace. Not that it's *any* of your business. He's considerate of me. Unlike some."

"He's lying. There's no way I could be alone with you in a room with a horizontal surface and not want to make love with you six ways till Sunday."

Tony regretted being so blunt. Maybe it was the thought of her in bed with Sterling that made him want to stake a claim. Or maybe it was because he'd been dreaming some pretty vivid stuff about her the past two nights.

Glancing around, he was glad to see the side street was all but deserted now.

Kat opened her mouth to say something, and all his good intentions deserted him. He silenced her with a kiss. Not too long, not too short, but with enough promise to back his words. After a moment of hesitation, she kissed him in return.

Kat tasted exactly as he'd expected, sweet and spicy, and about ready to burst into flames. Or maybe the flaming part was him.

Ending the kiss with a nibble on her lower lip, he rasped, "I take that back. There doesn't have to be a horizontal surface. I can be very creative with vertical spaces, too."

He regretted the words the minute they were out of his mouth. Judging from the horrified look on her face, she thought he had crossed a line. He knew he had.

Kat's cheeks flushed and she backed away from him.

He reached out to her. "I'm sorry, I shouldn't have done that."

"No, you shouldn't have. Because it'll be me who ends up getting hurt."

The vulnerability in her eyes underscored what a total bastard he'd been. He wanted to tell her he was different, that he wouldn't hurt her. But could he honestly make that claim? He was working this case for the Treadways, and getting involved with her was unacceptable. Being truthful impossible. Add a recent divorce that had left an aching hole in his life, and she'd be smart to keep her distance.

The knowledge didn't lessen the need that began in his groin and radiated to his chest. Or the crushing loneliness when he thought about his life back in Texas.

"You're absolutely right. I'm in no position to offer you anything." Yet he couldn't stand the thought of avoiding her. And his job required him to stay close to Sterling, who had given every indication of attaching himself to Kat. "But maybe we can be friends? I promise to behave."

Yeah, right, friends. With a woman he suddenly wanted more than air.

He kept his expression earnest, harmless. And felt only slightly guilty about lying to her. Why did he think he was any better than Sterling? Oh, yeah, because Tony wouldn't steal her money.

"You haven't told me to go screw myself. That's a good sign, right?" he asked, when she didn't reply.

Finally, she said, "Okay. But *only* if you behave."

Tony exhaled in relief.

Kat really *was* a crummy judge of character.

WILL PACED THE LENGTH of his suite, cursing under his breath.

What were the chances that he'd run into Mary Deveraux in tiny Jasper, Arizona? They'd met in some Midwest suburb at a beautiful lakeside resort. Illinois? Michigan? He couldn't remember. He did recall that she was a member of the Kansas City upper crust, recently widowed, grief-stricken and sitting on a pile of money. So he'd done what he did best—eased her grief and given her a reason to live again. The fact that he'd helped himself to most of her money over a six-month period was inconsequential. After all, Mary had willingly given him power of attorney. And if it weren't for him, she would have curled into a ball of self-pity and died. She should be grateful.

But after her verbal attack this afternoon, he realized she was another of a long line of women to betray him. She was obviously focused on materialism, forgetting how he'd come to her rescue. No wonder she was a bitter, lonely old woman.

There was a knock at the door. Peeking through the security viewer, he was gratified to see that it was Kat. She was earlier than he'd expected.

Going to the bed, he leaned against the headboard, wedging a pillow beneath his right foot and grabbing another to prop behind him.

"Come in," he called.

Kat peeked around the door. "I hope I'm not disturbing you. I wanted to check to make sure you were okay."

Grimacing, he motioned her inside. "You're not disturbing me. I'm sorry I had to leave you in the lurch today."

"I was fine." She sat on the bed next to him, though not nearly as close as he would have liked.

The sprained ankle was working. Kat was an obvious

caretaker, and there was no better way to make her feel good than to need her help.

She searched his face for signs of pain.

He winced almost imperceptibly.

Touching his calf, she asked, "Does it hurt a lot? Maybe you should go see a doctor."

He shifted forward on the pretense of rearranging the pillow behind his back. It put him close enough to feel her sweet breath on his face. Close enough to kiss her—except the time wasn't right.

"The pain's not unbearable. I've sprained my ankle before and know a doctor would only tell me to rest and apply ice. It'll be good as new in a couple days."

She stood and reached behind him, her cleavage tantalizingly near. "Lean toward me for a moment while I fluff your pillow."

Gladly.

Her hands were warm on his shoulders when she settled him back again. He could imagine her straddling him, naked, her gorgeous red hair tumbling down around them, her breathing erratic as he entered her—

A knock at the door interrupted his fantasy. A fantasy that surprised him in its intensity and vividness.

The interruption distracted Kat, too—which was probably a good thing. As she moved to the door, he shifted position, bending his left knee and bunching the covers over his lap so she wouldn't notice his obvious... interest.

The door opened wide and Tony Perez strode in as if he owned the place. The man had the worst timing.

Or…maybe his timing was intentional?

The hair on the back of Will's neck prickled. Perez wasn't sufficiently intelligent to be of any real threat to Will's plans.

Yet he seemed to turn up everywhere.

CHAPTER TWELVE

KAT TOOK A HIKE AFTER breakfast the next morning. It felt good to have time to herself in the natural beauty of the high Arizona desert.

She discovered a small valley where wildflowers still flourished late in the season. Bright yellow California poppies competed with lavender and pink blooms. The air was redolent with the sweet scent, along with desert sage and cypress.

Restless, she continued on, climbing where the trail grew more rocky and steep. Her breathing became uneven as she pushed herself. Sweat pooled between her breasts. It energized her to exercise out in the sunshine. She resolved to go hiking more often once she returned to her regular life in Tempe.

Twenty minutes into her climb, Kat found an outcropping of boulders just begging for her to sit and rest. She perched on the largest one, hoping there were no rattlesnakes sunning themselves on the other side.

She sipped from one of the water bottles she carried in holders looped through her belt. The icy liquid trickling down her throat was nearly erotic.

Taking in the view, Kat wished she'd brought her

camera. She tried to remember the last time she'd picked it up to do more than snap photos of friends, and realized it had to have been at least four years ago. Before she met Zach and he became the focus of her life.

A sense of loss constricted her chest. Surprisingly, not for losing Zach, but for the hobby she'd loved once upon a time. Another important piece of herself she'd given away to sustain a relationship that was never meant to be. The hollow ache was painfully insistent.

Kat wondered if she would ever meet a guy who didn't expect her to change, to mold herself into whoever he found most pleasing.

Tony's face came to mind, his clean, dark features and expressive eyes. The strength of his chin, not to mention his body, seemed to call to her. There was something else about him that drew her, and it irritated her that she hadn't been able to figure out what. Because if she could define it, she might have a better chance of resisting him.

Then there was Will. His face was blurry in her mind, like an old photo, faded and indistinct.

Both men had been glaringly absent at breakfast. Will had probably been eating in his room. And she had no idea where Tony had gone. He hadn't said a thing last night after he'd hurried her out of Will's room, much to the latter's irritation.

Breakfast with Lorraine and Lola had been almost peaceful without the two men engaging in a subtle testosterone contest.

Glancing at her watch, Kat realized she'd lost all track

NO POSTAGE
NECESSARY
IF MAILED
IN THE
UNITED STATES

BUSINESS REPLY MAIL
FIRST-CLASS MAIL   PERMIT NO. 717   BUFFALO, NY

POSTAGE WILL BE PAID BY ADDRESSEE

THE READER SERVICE
PO BOX 1867
BUFFALO NY 14240-9952

Send For
2 FREE BOOKS
Today!

I accept your offer!

Please send me two free
Harlequin® Superromance®
novels and two mystery
gifts (gifts worth about $10).
I understand that these books
are completely free—even
the shipping and handling will
be paid—and I am under no
obligation to purchase anything, ever,
as explained on the back of this card.

About how many NEW paperback fiction books have you purchased in the past 3 months?

❑ 0-2   ❑ 3-6   ❑ 7 or more
E7RH   **E7RT**   **E7R5**

❑ I prefer the regular-print edition   ❑ I prefer the larger-print edition
      135/336 HDL   **139/339 HDL**

Please Print

FIRST NAME

LAST NAME

ADDRESS

APT.#   CITY

Visit us online at
www.ReaderService.com

STATE/PROV.   ZIP/POSTAL CODE

► Detach card and mail today. No stamp needed. ► H-SR-07/10

Send For
2 FREE BOOKS
Today!

I accept your offer!

Please send me two free
Harlequin® Superromance®
novels and two mystery
gifts (gifts worth about $10).
I understand that these books
are completely free—even
the shipping and handling will
be paid—and I am under no
obligation to purchase anything, ever,
as explained on the back of this card.

**About how many NEW paperback fiction books have you
purchased in the past 3 months?**

❏ 0-2   ❏ 3-6   ❏ 7 or more
E7RH   **E7RT**   **E7R5**

❏ I prefer the regular-print edition   ❏ I prefer the larger-print edition
135/336 HDL   **139/339 HDL**

Please Print

FIRST NAME

LAST NAME

ADDRESS

APT.#   CITY

STATE/PROV.   ZIP/POSTAL CODE

Visit us online at
www.ReaderService.com

Offer limited to one per household and not valid to current subscribers of Harlequin® Superromance® books.
Your Privacy—Harlequin Books is committed to protecting your privacy. Our Privacy Policy is available online at
www.ReaderService.com or upon request from the Reader Service. From time to time we make our list of
customers available to reputable third parties who may have a product or service of interest to you. If you would
prefer for us not to share your name and address, please check here ❏. **Help us get it right**—We strive for
accurate, respectful and relevant communications. To clarify or modify your communication preferences, visit us at
www.ReaderService.com/consumerchoice.

of time and would have to hurry to shower before lunch. Surely Tony wouldn't miss two meals in a row?

TONY'S STOMACH GROWLED as he approached the Jasper town limits. He'd noticed a small, nondescript diner on the far side of the community yesterday. A tiny parking lot packed with cars and trucks attested to the quality of the food.

The hostess greeted him. "One? Is the bar okay?"

"Actually, I was hoping you could seat me at that booth in the corner. I like to keep my back to the wall." He flashed his most charming smile on the off chance she might refuse to waste a four-top on a lone guy.

He needn't have worried.

The heavyset waitress with tight salt-and-pepper curls merely nodded. "Law enforcement. No problem."

He didn't bother to correct her. Once law enforcement, always law enforcement, and some habits were impossible to break. He always carried a weapon, either in the glove compartment of his vehicle or an ankle holster, and he always sat with his back to the wall in a public restaurant.

It was a habit acquired during his first year as a Department of Public Safety officer, when a biker gang member executed a judge out to dinner with his family at a five-star restaurant. Even wearing biker colors, the perp and his partner had been in and out before anyone thought to stop them. And the judge's two kids were so traumatized they'd had to be hospitalized. As first responders, Tony and his partner had walked into a nightmare.

At least some good things had come out of Tony's retirement. He didn't have a string of new tragedies to add to all the old ones he'd investigated. Someday he might even regain a less cynical view of humanity.

The waitress came by and poured a cup of coffee, then took his order.

His scrambled eggs, sausage, bacon and Belgian waffle were delivered before he had time to get restless. He glanced around the restaurant. Sterling would probably stick out among the middle-aged hippies and artsy types that seemed to be regulars.

When the waitress brought his check, he pulled a couple of photos from his shirt pocket. "You ever see this man?" He handed her the picture of Will Sterling he'd surreptitiously taken with his cell phone.

"No, he's not from around here. Most of the locals eat here regular and I know them."

"How about this woman?" It was a long shot, but he had to try. Who knew where Eunice may have taken Will on vacation? He gave her a photo of Eunice Treadway provided by her son.

"No. Looks like a nice lady, though."

Tony nodded. "She was."

Just like the judge had been a nice man, before his head had been blown off for diligently doing his job. Sterling's methods were more indirect than the biker, but just as cruel. There was no doubt in Tony's mind that Sterling was morally responsible for Eunice's death.

Too bad the best he could hope for would be seeing him investigated and brought to trial for a string of less severe felonies: theft, fraud, manslaughter. Except manslaughter was a long shot even if they found evidence that Sterling had planted the idea of suicide in Eunice Treadway's mind.

After leaving the diner, Tony went next door to the bank and showed the photos to the manager, but she didn't recognize them. He debated a few other stops, but didn't want word to get around the small town.

Instead, he examined his map of downtown Jasper and found the Four Winds bed-and-breakfast. He walked up the hill toward it, gaining a better perspective of the town, dug into the side of a mountain, as he went.

A bell above the door jangled as he entered.

The interior was that of a rustic cottage, romantic, yet in keeping with the Wild West history of the town. A middle-aged man came through an entryway from what Tony assumed was a small office.

"I'm sorry, we're all booked up this week. But another nice bed-and-breakfast not far from here has vacancies."

Tony approached the desk. "I don't need a room at the moment, though I'll definitely keep you in mind for another time. I'm here to meet with Mary Deveraux."

"I'll call up to her room and let her know you're here. Your name?"

"Tony Perez. Please tell her it's important. It's in reference to Bill Powers."

The clerk punched in a few numbers and waited. "Mary, this is Tom at the front desk. There's a Tony Perez here to see you. He says it's important, in reference to Bill…"

"Powers," Tony repeated.

"Bill Powers." Tom listened for a moment. "You're sure? He had your name."

Tony shifted, wondering what she would say.

"I will." Tom replaced the receiver. His gaze was stern. "Ms. Deveraux doesn't know you or Bill Powers."

"She said that she didn't know Powers?"

"That's correct. I can't have you upsetting my guests. I'll have to ask you to leave."

"She was upset?"

Tom crossed his arms over his chest. "Yes, and very emphatic about not knowing either of you."

Rubbing his jaw, Tony thought for a second. "Here, how about I leave my card for Mrs. Deveraux? That way if she remembers Bill Powers, she can call me."

The man hesitated. "I guess there's no harm in that."

Pulling a business card out of his wallet, Tony bent over the desk, writing "Bill Powers, aka Will Sterling?" on the back. He handed it over along with a generous tip. "Thank you. I appreciate it."

"Keep your money. I'm the owner. I'll see that Mrs. Deveraux gets this."

"Thanks."

Tony walked outside, exhaling in disappointment.

He'd thought this might be the break he needed. With expenses mounting, the Treadway heirs would have been grateful. But it looked as if he'd have to return to Phoenix Rising and hope Sterling slipped up. And the only way that would work would be if Tony sat back while Kat put herself in harm's way.

He swore under his breath.

KAT FINISHED APPLYING the border to her journal with a glue gun.

Linda had commandeered the small conference room and converted it to a craft center this afternoon. She'd also commandeered Lola, Lorraine and several Red Hat Ladies relaxing at the resort until they attended a meeting in Jasper in two days.

"Are you done, Kat?" Linda asked.

"I think so."

The resort owner raised an eyebrow. "You don't sound too sure."

"I'm not. I haven't made a craft since vacation Bible school." She glanced at the Red Hat Ladies' creations, resplendent with red piping and purple sequins. "Mine isn't very fancy."

Linda came over and picked up Kat's journal. She'd chosen sage-green fabric for the cover, with a contrasting lavender cord attached as a bookmark. Then she'd drawn a sprinkling of desert wildflowers near the center of the front cover. "It's lovely. You've an artistic soul."

In spite of herself, Kat warmed at the praise. Her

mother hadn't spent much time with her since Kat's sister had announced her pregnancy.

"Thank you."

The rumble of a motorcycle prompted her to glance out the window just as Tony rode by. At least she assumed it was Tony; the rider wore a full face helmet.

A truly bad boy wouldn't wear a helmet; he would defy fate. Then whine pitifully when he wiped out in the rain and broke a leg, or worse. And of course lost his job as a result, because he couldn't work.

No, wait, that had been Zach.

Apparently truly devastating men wanted to keep their brains and bodies intact.

Linda had moved to the head of the table, counting out packets of stapled papers.

"This is your assignment." She chuckled. "I bet you didn't realize there would be homework."

One of the Red Hat Ladies clapped her hands. "I love homework."

Suck up. Still Kat smiled at the woman's enthusiasm. She couldn't imagine having the patience to sit down and pour out her heart on paper.

Her reluctance must have shown on her face, because Linda said, "My daughter prefers to journal with her laptop. Then she can cut and paste snippets to exchange with friends on her social networking site."

Kat nodded. Now that made sense. She accepted the handout for Linda, thinking she might set up a journal in a Word file.

As she stood to leave, she heard the other ladies

pepper Linda with questions about social networking sites.

When Kat returned to her casita, she opened her laptop and booted it up. She intended to start a journal file, but got sidetracked with e-mail, her mother's response first in the queue. She rolled her eyes when she saw a link to the baby countdown on her sister's Facebook page. And tried not to feel guilty that she couldn't handle being there until after the baby was born. She would find a way to make it up to Nicole later.

Still no response from her father. Even though she'd lived with him after the divorce, the abandonment she now felt was familiar. As was her instinct to rationalize why he hadn't come through for her yet again. Was an e-mail every once in a while too much to ask?

Apparently so.

But Kat suspected there was something wrong. It was a gut feeling more than anything else.

She fired off e-mails to her mom and stepmother, Sharon, asking if there was a reason Dad hadn't been in touch. Then she sat back and waited for a response.

CHAPTER THIRTEEN

AT PHOENIX RISING THAT evening, Tony slipped into a seat at a table by the door, ten minutes late for dinner. The waiter took his order and brought a salad.

Shaking out his napkin, Tony introduced himself to the four others at the table, two couples in their late twenties who soon lapsed into a conversation that didn't include him, about a recent high school reunion.

It was just as well, because Tony wasn't in the mood for polite conversation. He was frustrated with his lack of progress on the Treadway case. Glancing around the room, he easily located Kat by her red hair. But instead of her normal riot of curls, her hair fell to her shoulders in a smooth, straight wave. He wondered how she'd managed to pull off that trick.

For some reason, the change annoyed him. He *liked* her hair curly and wild.

And next to her sat Will, his crutches propped in the corner nearby.

Will whispered something in Kat's ear. Then he kissed her bare shoulder, above the colorful floral print dress she wore.

Tony's mood darkened further when she laughed

and affectionately touched Will's arm, as if he was the most wonderful man in the world.

Fortunately, the entrée was served and Tony had to concentrate on his salmon. But his attention wandered to the table in the corner every time he heard Kat's laugh. Will's leg appeared fused to hers beneath the table. Which brought to mind other ways in which they could be fused together tonight, an image that ruined Tony's appetite.

Tossing down his napkin, he excused himself and strode to their table.

He tapped Kat's left shoulder.

Turning, she raised her face to meet his gaze, her lips upturned.

"I, um, was wondering if I missed anything while I was gone today?"

Smooth, Perez.

Kat frowned. "Not really. Unless you had a burning desire to decorate a journal so you could explore your innermost feelings at a later date. Linda roped me into a journal-crafting class with some visiting Red Hat Ladies."

"Hell, no!" He shuddered. "Not that I have anything against Red Hat Ladies."

Chuckling, she responded, "I didn't think so. But if you change your mind about the journaling part, I have the handout to guide you in digging deep."

"Maybe I could get it from you later this evening? My mom wants to write her memoirs, and that might be a good way for her to start," he lied. Well, he vaguely remembered his mother saying something about wanting to get family lore down on paper, but hadn't paid much attention at the time. It had seemed like one more idea to help fill her time since his dad died two years ago, leaving her alone in the big San Antonio ranch-style home he'd grown up in.

"Sure."

Tony threw Sterling a look. That ought to put a cramp in any seduction plans for this evening. He was willing to bet Will's motives were to get into Kat's panties, then her bank account, in that order.

And what were Tony's motives? If he was putting his client first, he'd allow nature to take its course. And would quit trying to compete with Sterling.

What would happen if, for once, Tony didn't put his work first? It was a question he didn't want to ask himself. Because the thought of getting Kat into bed was more tempting than he could have imagined.

Tony watched Kat's face grow animated as she described the other class attendees. He nodded in the appropriate places even though he was distracted.

Running his hand through his hair, he longed for the days when he'd been married and on the force. Policy and his wedding vows, along with the knowledge that Corrine was a crack shot, had kept him on the straight and narrow.

Now he only had his own sense of right and wrong. Which seemed to be deserting him where Kat was concerned.

He was screwed....

Linda saved him from any more introspection by stopping at their table, clipboard in hand.

Tony used the diversion to try to slip away before she could corral him into some stupid activity. Although he had to admit the glassblowing had been great.

"Tony, don't go sneaking off." She beckoned him with a languid wave of her hand. "I expect you to be the first to sign up for this evening's surprise event."

Damn. Too slow.

"What am I volunteering for? Please tell me there's no journaling involved."

Linda laughed. "Kat told you. No, tonight we're having a test run for a new activity we hope to offer. We're coordinating with a neighboring stable to have a moonlit trail ride. The stable will provide the horses and a guide. Phoenix Rising provides wine and cheese and some other goodies for a picnic when you reach your destination. We thought it might be an event the camp children might enjoy this summer, sans the wine and with more adult supervision, of course."

His interest piqued in spite of himself, he asked, "And where is the destination?"

"That's for me to know and you to find out." The sparkle in her eyes told him he didn't want to miss this. And it would benefit at-risk children, a win-win if there ever was one.

His opinion was confirmed when Kat exclaimed, "I love to ride. It'll be fun."

"Yeah, fun," he parroted, watching the way the layers of her hair caressed her cheek and reflected the overhead light. A few strands caught at the corner of her mouth and he was tempted to brush them away with a kiss.

"Kat, I was hoping you and I could have a quiet evening…alone," Will said in a low voice.

"But this will be great! I haven't ridden since high school." Kat grasped his hand. "We can still spend time together at the picnic."

"I'm a very accomplished horseman. But—" he gestured helplessly at his right foot "—I'm in no condition to ride. It's so disappointing."

Her eyes were shadowed. "I don't want to leave you here by yourself…."

If Sterling was any sort of a man, he'd tell her to have a good time, and he'd watch a game on TV while she was gone.

But he simply allowed her sentence to trail off. Manipulative bastard.

Kat's shoulders slumped. "Linda, I'm going to stay here with Will."

Tony was probably the only one who saw Sterling suppress his delight. Though it was tempting to leave the jerk behind, he had to watch him in action. "What about a wagon?" he asked. "Will could ride in one of those and not have to miss out on all the fun."

"Thanks for thinking of me, Perez. But I don't want to put these folks to any trouble."

"It's no trouble at all. I should have thought of it myself." Linda nodded, writing something on her clipboard. "We have a small wagon that carries the picnic supplies. Will can ride shotgun. That'll make twelve people total. Plus there would be room for Lorraine and Lola in the wagon, too. I bet they'd enjoy that."

"Sounds great." Will's voice was overly hearty as he glared daggers at Tony.

It was hard for Tony to keep from gloating. He'd have Kat to himself while Will rode in the wagon like a little girl.

WILL SEETHED. How dare they treat him like some frail old woman. He was supposed to be injured, not pathetic. But Perez smirked as Will carefully climbed up on the wagon. Thank goodness Lorraine and Lola had declined, or he'd have had to endure their endless chatter. As it was, the dust alone would make it less than enjoyable.

Kat was already mounted on a beautiful tan horse with a blond mane. She seemed relaxed and happy.

Will felt cheated. This was supposed to be the night they became lovers. He'd been looking forward to it all day. Especially because, despite her flashes of wildness, his instincts told him Kat was the type of monogamous woman who totally invested herself in a man once she was intimate. Once he brought her to orgasm, she'd be his for as long as he cared to keep her around. And Will was beginning to think he'd like that to be a very long time.

If Perez didn't interfere with his plans, that is. The man swung himself up in the saddle, seemingly unafraid of the huge red animal that pranced beneath him. He clicked his tongue and the horse settled.

Will was irritated to note that Kat followed Perez's movements, too.

But Will wasn't that worried. He still had a few tricks up his sleeve. Kat would be his before Perez knew what hit him.

KAT INHALED THE FRESH scent of cedar as they followed the mounted guide single file. The full moon above shed plenty of light to see the well-maintained trail that sloped gently upward through the manzanita and scrub. It was wonderful to be riding again. Their mounts were gentle trail horses for the most part, with the exception of Tony's sorrel gelding. Its curved neck and delicate ankles hinted at Arabian ancestry. Tony handled the fidgety animal with confidence and ease.

Kat's palomino mare, Buttercup, was sweet-tempered, but with enough energy in her stride to suggest she might enjoy a gallop. Not now, though.

Turning her horse, Kat headed toward the back of the line, where the wagon lagged behind. She brought her horse alongside Will. "How's your leg doing?"

"It's…" he winced as the wagon hit a rut "—okay. I wish I was riding with you."

"Do you ride English or Western?"

He hesitated for a split second. "English, of course. That's where the real skill comes into play."

"I don't know about that." Kat raised her chin. "Western requires plenty of skill, too."

He smiled, waving away their difference of opinion. "Why don't we just agree to disagree?"

Kat's mare got restless after a few minutes of plodding next to the wagon. Probably picking up on her rider's mood.

"It seems like this little lady needs to work off some energy. If you don't mind, I'll catch up with the rest and see you at the picnic?"

He frowned. "I'd hoped you'd stay here with me."

She hesitated, resentment simmering. "I will, if you really want me to. But I haven't ridden in years and it's heavenly for me to get this chance...."

"Go. I'll be fine."

"You're sure?"

"Absolutely." Will saluted her. "Save me a spot on your picnic blanket."

Kat laughed, relieved. He really was a great guy. "Of course."

Clicking her tongue, she touched her heels to the mare's sides. That was all it took for her mount to spring into action, trotting for a second before moving into a rolling canter.

Kat, laughing with sheer joy, felt as if she was flying. She hadn't been this free since the summer she turned fifteen, when her childhood had effectively ended.

Spotting the sorrel stopped ahead at the side of the path, she slowed her mare. "Waiting for someone?"

"Yeah, for you." Tony's smile was crooked. She could have almost sworn she heard him murmur, "All my life."

She figured the breeze was playing tricks on her. "You handle your mount well. How long have you been riding?"

"I'm a native Texan. I rode with my parents before I could walk. You?"

"I started riding in junior high. Our subdivision was next to horse properties and one of them boarded horses. I worked there during the summers, mucking stalls, feeding, grooming and exercising the animals. I loved it."

"I can tell." He leaned toward her. "Your eyes sparkle when you talk about it."

"It's dark. You can't see my eyes that well."

"There's a full moon. I can see them sparkle from here, darlin'."

The way his tongue wrapped around the endearment was almost sinful. Awareness tingled on every nerve ending in her body. Oh, this was so not the time to lust for the wrong guy.

"I think you've got a vivid imagination."

"That, too."

Kat laughed. "Don't agree with me. I don't know how to handle it."

"You're not easy to please."

"On the contrary, I'm *very* easy to please." She hadn't meant her teasing remark to have a double meaning, but realized how it sounded the minute it came out of her mouth. "I meant, in general terms."

"I knew exactly what you meant. And there's nothing general about the ways I could please you." He glanced from the top of her head, where she could feel the breeze playing with her straightened hair, past the form-fitting, blue-and-white-striped, cotton blouse, to her low-slung jeans. "I like this look."

A smile tugged at his mouth when her cheeks grew warm. She shouldn't encourage his flirtation. But it was fun to play these go-away-closer games with a gorgeous man.

It had been way too long.

And she was tired of being cautious.

CHAPTER FOURTEEN

KAT SLOWED THE MARE. It was as if riding again had taken her back to her teen years, where she had felt anything was possible. When she'd believed there was a Prince Charming out there waiting for her.

But with maturity had come the painful realization that Prince Charming existed only in fairy tales. And maybe in her friend Annie's marriage.

Kat had turned a corner in her life and she had no intention of backsliding. Stability was what she needed, and Tony Perez was not the kind of man who would give her the house and white picket fence. He'd eventually leave when he realized she wasn't as together as she wanted everyone to believe.

Besides, he was too confident. Too self-contained. Even his playful innuendos seemed carefully thought out. He did fine on his own and didn't need anyone. Least of all her. And that made him more dangerous than any bad boy.

Kat never felt more cherished than when a man needed her. It made her special. She suspected Will was the kind of man who would cherish her if she gave him the chance, if she could just let go with him the way she craved to let go with Tony.

Glancing over her shoulder, she saw Will's somber expression. Her heart lurched. He seemed so alone. She felt a pull of attraction to Will, as if somehow the puzzle pieces of her stubborn heart were shifting into place.

"He's fine." Tony moved his horse alongside hers. Her mare pranced a bit, pretending to shy, before settling down.

"I feel bad for him."

"Don't. He'll survive. His kind always does."

"What do you mean, 'his kind'?"

"He's a user, Kat. It's what he does. He'll always land on his feet. Both of them." Tony's gaze was direct, all playfulness gone.

"You don't even know him."

He opened his mouth as if to say something, then clamped it shut. A few minutes later, his voice was low when he said, "I know enough, okay?"

Kat was tempted to ignore his statement. Pretend she hadn't heard. But, no, dammit, he had to understand she couldn't be manipulated simply because he had a different agenda. She straightened her spine. "I make my own decisions about people."

His mouth twisted in a frown. "And I'm sure you're usually right. But people like Will don't play by the same rules as the rest of us."

The trail narrowed and Kat urged Buttercup ahead of the gelding, grateful to end their conversation. Grateful that he was behind her and couldn't see the effect his warning had on her, jumbling her thoughts. Her instincts told her he was keeping something from her. Something important.

It was similar to the feeling she'd gotten as a teen when her dad had an unexpected business meeting or trip that lasted longer than anticipated. As if there was an undercurrent she might understand if only she tried harder. But no matter how many questions she asked, her father evaded a definitive discussion. Kat always felt the answer was just beyond her reach. And she'd end up abandoned again, because she wasn't smart enough to figure it out.

"At least think about what I've said," Tony called.

She nodded, if for no other reason than to get him to ease up. He'd given her way too much to think about already. She kept her back ramrod straight.

They rode in silence, the sound of the horses' hooves leaching away her tension. Horses had been her salvation in those awful days when there had been so much fighting at home. She'd escape to the stable every afternoon and on weekends, forgetting for a while how precarious her world seemed. Forgetting the circumstances she was certain she could control if only she understood the subtext of her parents' whispered disagreements and stony silences.

She'd taken every opportunity to enjoy the peace of the stables, the comfort of a warm muzzle nibbling her palm, of an animal never expecting more than she could give. Until her parents had divorced and there was too much to do at home. She'd taken on the lion's share of the cooking, cleaning and laundry, since her dad had seemed so lost in the days following the death of his marriage. Soon, he took for granted that Kat would keep the house running while he was away doing whatever he was doing.

She hadn't realized until now how much she'd given up. Or how little thanks she'd received. A shaft of insight seared her with painful intensity. She'd given up her childhood and childish dreams for her father; her adulthood and grown-up dreams had been handed over to one undeserving man after another.

Coincidence?

An excited exclamation from the rider ahead gave Kat the excuse she needed to break off her thoughts. She strained to see around him. As he rode on, she saw that the trail opened up into a meadow, cast in silver from the full moon that hung low in the sky.

"It's beautiful," she breathed.

Two deer raised their heads from grazing and bounded off into the deep shadows of the trees.

The guests followed the guide into the center of the opening. Nobody spoke. It was as if the meadow was a magical place.

The spell was broken a few minutes later when the wagon lumbered into the clearing, creaking with every dip and rock until the driver reined in the horses.

Tammy, a wiry woman with a long gray braid hanging down her back, dismounted from her horse. "Beautiful spot, isn't it?"

Without waiting for an answer, she handed her reins

to Tony and went over to the wagon, unloading supplies while she barked instructions to a young cowboy, presumably her son. An older, grizzled man stepped down from the driver's seat of the wagon and pitched in.

Large pieces of canvas were spread out on the ground, separated by several feet. Close enough to feel connected, yet far enough to carry on a private conversation.

"You know how to tie off a horse?" Tammy asked Tony.

"Yes, ma'am." His Texas drawl sounded more pronounced.

"I can, too," Kat offered as she dismounted.

"Good. You can tie the horses to that small stand of trees over there." She pointed to about ten trees that looked as if they'd been dropped about the length of a football field away.

She raised her voice so it would carry. "The rest of you ride over to those trees, and Tony and Kat will tie off your mounts for you."

Kat's thighs protested as she swung back into the saddle and trotted her mare to the grove. She knew she would be sore tomorrow, but it was well worth it. Being around horses again made her feel alive. Helping did, too.

"You haven't stopped smiling, except to give me a hard time."

"I didn't give you a hard time."

Tony guided his horse close. This time Buttercup

didn't even pretend to shy. She simply nickered and nuzzled the sorrel's nose.

If only it was that easy to trust in humans.

Tony's knee jostled Kat's. "You're going to picnic with me, aren't you?"

She wouldn't meet his gaze. It almost felt as if she was cheating. "I think Will wanted me to hang out with him."

"Do you really want that?"

"Maybe. I'm not sure." She surprised herself with her honesty. The last thing she wanted to do was start opening up to Tony.

He reached over and placed his hand on hers where she held the reins. "Just promise me you'll be careful."

She nodded, pulling her hands and reins out of his grasp.

They reached the trees and dismounted, tying off their horses. The other riders came over and dismounted one by one.

Kat and Tony worked in tandem as if they'd been a team forever. Between the two of them, they were able to make sure the horses couldn't wander off.

When they'd finished they walked slowly back to the picnic area.

"You sound serious when you warn me about Will." She tucked her hair behind her ears. "Tell me what you know."

"I can't."

"Why not?"

"I can't even tell you that."

Kat wanted him to give her a reason to trust him. "You can't go around making cryptic remarks about a man and not back them up. Not if you want me to take you seriously."

"I'd hoped my word would be enough."

"We barely know each other."

His gaze was steady, searching. "I think we've spent enough time together for you to figure out I'm not one of the bad guys. If you still think that, there's nothing I can do to change your mind."

"Being honest would be a start. There's something you're not telling me and that doesn't inspire a lot of confidence. I don't like secrets."

Tony stopped. His voice was low and tense as he said. "Kat, I have my reasons for not telling you everything. But I wouldn't intentionally hurt you. Have a little faith when I say I have your best interests at heart."

Clearing her throat, Kat turned her head. Otherwise he might see the tears she furiously blinked away. His sincerity made her waver. Wasn't that what she'd always wanted a man to say? That he put her interests above his own. That he'd protect her with his last breath.

Kat wanted that and more. She wanted the truth.

And Tony wasn't offering the whole package. He talked about faith and good intentions, but what did he back it up with? Evasions and half-truths. His dedication to her, if it was sincere, would surely change. It might take months, maybe even years, but he'd get that glassy, distracted expression that told her she simply wasn't enough. Even now he was offering empty reassurances only a fool would believe.

Her days of being a fool had ended when she'd asked Zach for her key and sent him packing.

She shook off Tony's hand now. "I lost my faith in men a long time ago. You'll have to give me cold, hard facts."

He slid his hand behind her neck, his eyes darkening with emotion. "I wish I could."

Kat wanted to do something stupid, like to press his callused palm to her cheek and tell him she believed him. But she couldn't.

Borrowing a phrase from Will, she almost achieved a light tone when said, "Then it looks like we'll have to agree to disagree."

What she really meant was that there couldn't be anything between them. Judging by the tense line of his mouth, Tony got the message loud and clear.

Pulling away, Kat approached the center of the meadow, where an old fire pit was stacked with wood and kindling.

She shivered, rubbing her arms, telling herself the night air had chilled her. But she suspected it was the loss of something she'd never had to begin with.

She felt Tony step behind her.

He didn't touch her, didn't speak. But his presence reached out to her. And she couldn't respond.

"Kat," Will called, "over here."

She was determined to do things right this time. She walked away from Tony without a backward glance.

WILL SHIFTED uncomfortably. Sitting on the ground wasn't his idea of fun. The only reason he was here walked toward him, looking sexy in a pair of jeans and casual striped cotton blouse, her expression mysterious in the moonlight. Almost someone he might see in one of the more romantic Chaps advertisements.

Smiling in welcome at the same time he imagined her naked, Will stood and greeted her with a kiss on the cheek. Possession was nine-tenths of the law, or so the saying went.

"You look beautiful. Very…earthy."

She smiled, her teeth straight and white. Their children would have great teeth. He could almost imagine the Christmas cards they would send, complete with a photo of their perfect family.

"Thank you…I think." She brushed back her hair. "Do I have dirt on my face?"

He chuckled. "I meant earthy in a more…sensual way. Brimming with energy and sex appeal."

"Why, thank you." She wrinkled her nose and grinned. "You'll probably think I smell earthy, too. And I mean that in the horsey way."

"I'll take my chances. Make yourself comfortable. We have a picnic basket full of stuff." After gesturing toward it, he sat within arm's reach of the food. He intended to make this a night to remember. For both of them.

TONY LEANED AGAINST THE wagon as he polished off the last of his dinner. He'd declined the wine and cheese selection, instead having fried chicken and potato salad with the stable staff. The meal had been top-notch, washed down with a cold beer.

He listened to the old cowboy, George, deliver the punch line to his story. Tony laughed in the appropriate places, but kept his eye on Kat the entire time.

The longer the evening went on, the more restless he got. Especially since the distance between Will and Kat seemed to diminish over the course of the picnic. He was afraid the wine might be lowering her resistance to the con man's dubious charm.

George nudged him with his elbow. "Why don't you go over there and stake your claim?"

"What do you mean?"

"I've seen the way you watch the pretty redhead. Looks like the city guy is moving in on your territory. Can't let that happen."

"Kat's not my territory. I just don't want her to get hurt."

George shook his head, chewing on a toothpick. "And here I'd heard Texans had balls."

The comment rankled, as was intended. "We do. But there are times when it's better to sit back and observe. 'Know when to hold 'em, know when to fold 'em,' as the song says."

"I guess you know what you're doing." George's tone clearly held doubt. "Besides, we'll be setting up chairs around the fire before too long. Linda wants to sing songs."

Tony chuckled. "Like we're her at-risk campers. Is she for real?"

"Nice lady. Her and her husband both. Good neighbors. They bought that land at auction for cents on the dollar. Hired local crews for the construction. Then did a lot of the finish work themselves."

"It must be a hard living, making the resort pay." Tony placed his paper plate and plastic utensils in the garbage bag, his beer can in the sack designated for recyclables.

"Don't need to. The way I hear it, Garth makes more money than he could ever spend with that glass art stuff, so they were looking for a tax write-off. The resort has always been Linda's dream."

"Interesting." And it was. Tony could have chatted with the old guy for hours…except he noticed Will lean in and kiss Kat on the lips.

"Sorry, George, I think you're right. I better go visit those two." He nodded in the direction of Kat and Will, who were still kissing.

"Go on."

Tony strode over to their blanket. "Mind if I hang out till the sing-along starts?" Only it came out more demand than question. He didn't intend to take no for an answer.

CHAPTER FIFTEEN

MIXED EMOTIONS WASHED OVER Kat when Tony joined them. Less than an hour earlier she couldn't get away from him fast enough, and now her spirits lifted at his presence. Her roller coaster feelings were confusing.

Maybe it was because Will seemed to be moving in quickly, hinting about spending the night together. Kat simply wasn't ready for that with him. Apparently she needed time to develop that kind of bond with a nice guy. Maybe that's how solid, long-lasting relationships were forged?

Will was irritated bordering on rude at Tony's interruption. She couldn't really blame him. "We were having a private moment here."

"*Were* is the operative word." Tony sat next to her.

Clearing her throat, she said, "He shouldn't have to eat by himself, Will."

"He wasn't by himself."

"And the ranch hands had some interesting stories. But now I'd like to hang out with the two of you."

The thought of these men being friends who hung out made Kat nearly laugh. The contrast had never been more apparent. Tony, dressed in faded Wranglers that molded to his muscular thighs and narrow hips; scuffed, old cowboy boots on his feet. He radiated good humor. The determined tilt to his jaw was the only evidence that he meant business.

Will wore khaki chinos, a royal-blue golf shirt and previously ultrawhite tennis shoes that were looking decidedly less pristine. His chinos were covered in trail dust and would probably never come clean. She suspected he'd been exaggerating his experience to impress her. Anyone who had ridden a horse had to know dirt was a given.

"You said something about a sing-along?" Kat asked, eager for a group activity. The sexual tension was getting too thick for her comfort.

"Yes. George said they'll bring out the folding chairs and group them around the fire pit for an old-fashioned sing-along, while we toast marshmallows for s'mores."

"We could have used those chairs over an hour ago, instead of sitting on the ground." Will rubbed his backside.

Tony raised an eyebrow. "But then it wouldn't seem like a picnic. You don't hear Kat complaining."

His manhood in question, Will clamped his mouth shut.

Tony moved closer to Kat. She noticed how the lantern light danced along the planes of his face, highlighting his straight nose and strong chin.

In turn, he studied her. The silence stretched longer

than was appropriate, but for the life of her, Kat couldn't look away.

Will cleared his throat.

Trying to cover her confusion, she asked, "What, do I have food in my teeth?"

"No… I was thinking you look very at home in this environment. More veteran horsewoman than accountant."

Kat tilted her head. She found Tony's observation… flattering. Lately she'd grown restless with her job. "I used to like my work because it was predictable. Other parts of my life weren't, so it was nice when one and one always added up to two. Not so many gray areas."

"And now?" Will asked, inserting himself in the conversation.

She plucked a blade of grass and rolled it between her thumb and forefinger. "Now I'm reassessing a lot of things. But being a CPA is lucrative and I can't just walk away. Especially since I'm good at what I do."

"Yeah, I thought that once about a career," Tony interjected. "It's amazing what you can manage when life puts you between a rock and a hard place."

"Your career before you were a consultant?"

He nodded.

She opened her mouth to ask more, when Will said, "I've always loved my work as a life coach. It's fulfilling to see the changes I make in people's lives."

"I bet." It was as if Tony was trying to antagonize Will.

Kat felt compelled to buffer the tension. "I think it

sounds intriguing." Practically batting her eyelashes, she continued, "And it's wonderful you can help people."

Tony remained blessedly silent. He was obviously confident and self-assured. He'd probably always been picked first for dodgeball, excelled in academics, and been captain of the football team in high school. He'd never been the underdog like Will. Or her.

Kat had always had a soft spot for the underdog, probably because she'd experienced a stretch of social awkwardness herself. Her popularity hadn't started till midway into her high school career, when she'd lost her gangliness and braces. And learned to dumb herself down to get attention. Selective promiscuity and a penchant to cancel dates at a moment's notice to take care of her dad only added to her mysterious allure.

Will laced his fingers through hers and rested them on his knee. "Like you, I've been told I'm very good at what I do. It sounds as if you're at the perfect point to benefit from a life coach."

Not wanting to hurt his feelings, she said, "I'll think about it."

"Looks like they're setting up the chairs." Tony unfolded his tall frame and stood, holding his hand out to her.

She accepted his help, slightly self-conscious because Will had been holding her hand just moments before.

Will stood, favoring his right leg.

Kat hurried to his side. "I completely forgot about your ankle." She wrapped her arm around his waist.

"Here, lean on me. We should have gotten you a chair from the start."

"What happened to your crutches?" Tony frowned.

"Useless on this uneven ground." Will stared as if challenging him to refute his logic.

Tony shrugged. "Move over, Kat. I've got him. You might hurt yourself."

Before she knew it, Kat was standing on the sideline, watching two men who obviously didn't like each other make their way toward the fire pit.

She bit her lip, feeling as if she should do something, anything, to help.

But before she knew it, Tony had deposited Will in a lawn chair and was practically dusting his hands together. Mission accomplished.

Kat knew a lot of women who found take-charge men attractive. She'd never been one of them. Because nothing less than perfection would do for the woman in his life. Her father was a prime example.

And Kat had learned early on she was far from perfect.

At least with Zach the issue had never come up. She'd always been too focused on getting him out of one scrape after another.

TONY WAS FRUSTRATED the rest of the evening. Kat hovered over Will, getting him a drink from the cooler, asking if he wanted to ice his ankle.

It was enough to make Tony want to hurl.

The more she pampered, the more smug the SOB got. And the angrier Tony became.

He told himself the best, really the only way at this point, to gain information was to sit back and watch Sterling work Kat. Watch how he gained her confidence, note any patterns, any similarities to what he knew about Sterling's M.O. with Eunice. Even the smallest tidbit of information could be useful.

But inside he still seethed. As far as Kat was concerned this evening, Tony apparently didn't exist, except in small, isolated instances. What was up with that? He was reasonably good-looking, worked out regularly, could make conversation with almost anyone, and loved God and country. Whereas Will was a snake in the grass, though he managed to conceal the fact for the most part.

Shaking his head, Tony realized for the millionth time he would never understand women. What's more, he should stop trying. Until the next time Kat smiled in his direction. Then all bets were off.

When Linda opened the bag of marshmallows, Tony remembered overhearing Kat say how much she liked s'mores. Surely the lure of toasting marshmallows and chocolate would coax her over.

No such luck.

Grabbing two coat hangers, he held them in the flame to burn off any chemical residue. After they cooled, he loaded two marshmallows on each. He made sure to brown them slowly so they wouldn't burn. When they were toasted, he went to the supply table, grabbed a packet of graham crackers and some chocolate bars and took them to Kat.

She and Will were laughing about some private joke when he walked up. They looked altogether too cozy with their lawn chairs right next to each other.

Tony knew he shouldn't let their developing relationship get to him. He should be above personal involvement.

Yeah, right.

Since he'd failed miserably in the personal involvement arena, he would simply have to become a better actor. Even if he seethed on the inside, he needed to temper his response on the outside.

He handed the supplies to her, along with a handful of napkins. "I thought you might like to try a s'more."

"I love s'mores." She jumped up to inspect the marshmallows. "Perfect."

Tony's chest expanded with her praise, as if he'd single-handedly slain a woolly mammoth and dragged it back to the cave for her.

As she assembled the treat, he watched her lick a drop of melted chocolate off her wrist. The sight of her tongue capturing it made his groin tighten.

On impulse, he leaned close. "Next time let me get that for you, darlin'."

She smacked him on the biceps. "Behave yourself."

Then she offered half to Will.

Tony felt as if she'd regifted his heart.

"Thanks, but I'm trying to cut back on refined sugar," Sterling said.

Kat shrugged, her smile fading.

Tony cocked his head. Somebody needed to take this guy down a peg.

Detachment, Perez, detachment.

He managed a teasing tone. "Girl and Boy Scouts have subsisted on s'mores during camping trips for decades. Surely you're not maligning the sacred tradition of Scouting?"

"I wasn't a Boy Scout."

"Who'd have thought?" He turned to Kat. "Were you a Girl Scout?"

"Absolutely. After I graduated from Brownies."

"I thought so. I almost made Eagle Scout. Except once I hit junior high my...interests changed."

"What, they didn't offer a badge for shoveling horse manure?" Will echoed Tony's teasing tone of moments ago.

"Actually," Kat said, "the Girl Scouts did. I earned a horsemanship badge for working at a neighboring stable for a weekend. Later, in high school, I worked there a lot. And believe me, I shoveled plenty of manure."

"See, the difference there, Kat, is that you and I shoveled shit when we were kids." Tony could feel his hostility toward Sterling build, along with the desire to kick his ass. "Some people start shoveling it as adults."

Tony thought he'd managed a mild, nonconfrontational tone until he saw Kat's shoulders tense.

CHAPTER SIXTEEN

KAT TRIED TO AVOID TONY once she got Will settled in the wagon, his leg propped on a nest of canvas. The competition between the two men made it impossible for her to enjoy herself. And try as she might, she couldn't get Tony's warnings out of her mind.

Were they merely jealousy? The uncertainty put her nerves on edge.

Swinging up on the mare's back, she made sure to fall into the line moving single file down the hillside, with at least one horse as a buffer between her and Tony's sorrel.

She had just started to relax again when the trail widened and she heard hooves approaching quickly from behind.

Without looking over her shoulder Kat knew it was Tony.

"Hey." He reined in his horse and fell in beside her. "You're not trying to avoid me, are you?"

"You were rude to Will. I don't like rude people. It shows a genuine lack of concern, as if what you want counts more than what someone else wants."

That had surely been the case with Zach. He'd been

rude to anyone who expressed an opinion counter to his. Especially when it had been Kat expressing the opinion. Come to think of it, her father had become dismissive if she didn't agree with him, as if it were a personal betrayal. He would freeze her out, become distant, spend more time away from home.

"Even if they're telling the truth?"

A high cloud filtered the moonlight for a moment and Kat concentrated on the trail ahead, even though her horse probably knew every inch.

When her eyes adjusted, she demanded, "How can you accuse Will of lying when you don't know the man? Just because he's not as macho as you are doesn't automatically make him evil."

"No, his actions make him evil. You'll just have to take my word that you should stay away from him."

Oh, yes, this sounded *very* familiar.

"Take *your* word? I don't know you. And who decreed you the great judge of right and wrong?"

"I was almost an Eagle Scout." His crooked grin was nearly her undoing. As was the pressure to pretend conflict never happened—again Zach's M.O.

It would be so easy to ignore the red flags and have a fling with him. But she was not a fling kind of woman. Even in her wilder days, her promiscuity had mostly been for show—setting herself apart from the nerds. And a misguided attempt to become indispensable to her boyfriend du jour. Love had very little to do with it.

"'Almost' only counts in horseshoes and hand

grenades," she observed tartly, studying him. "You made a snap judgment about Will and weren't very nice to him. I hate it when people pick on someone because he's different."

"Just a wild guess here, but I bet you rescue people. Men, in particular."

She refused to answer.

"I was right." But there wasn't any triumph in his voice. Only regret. He nudged his horse closer, till his thigh brushed hers. It felt…right. "Darlin' you deserve so much more than that. You should have a strong man who works hard to make sure you're happy. A man who'd give his life for you."

Blinking back tears, Kat decided she needed to get away from him and fast. He was more dangerous than she had imagined. He was describing the kind of man she'd always wanted, but could never have. Glancing around wildly, she looked for an escape. But she was hemmed in by riders in front and behind. And on her right was thick scrub scattered with large boulders.

With nowhere to run, she refused to back down. "And I suppose you're that man? Not hardly. At least Will is a gentleman and cares about my feelings."

"Oh, I care all right. That's why I can't sit back and watch you make a fool of yourself."

That did it. Fury burned her cheeks. He saw through her so easily.

"*Nobody* makes a fool of me."

Kat ached to smack him, not only for his audacity, but also his insight. She was such a liar. To Tony, but mostly to herself. Zach had made a fool of her. And the boyfriend before him. And pretty much every boyfriend since she'd started dating in junior high. The only man who hadn't made a fool of her was her father. And that was one of the many reasons she'd idolized him all of her adult life. Even as she'd resented how little he gave. No man could ever measure up.

Her stomach churned as loss melded with anger. Kat blinked, irritated beyond measure because she wanted to bawl instead of tearing Tony a new one.

"Hey, I didn't mean to make you cry. I…just don't want to see you hurt. It's…none of my business, and I'll butt out. Scout's honor."

"It's not only you…it's everything."

The path widened even more as they rounded the bend to the stables. The horses' ears swiveled forward, and the mare mouthed her bit, anticipating oats after a job well done.

Kat loosened the reins and tapped Buttercup with her heels. That was all the encouragement needed. Soon they were flying effortlessly, barely touching the ground. Moonlight painted a surreal path, all inky blue punctuated by silver and black.

Kat wished with all her heart she was the person Tony thought her to be. A woman worthy of being cherished by a man.

AFTER THANKING THE STABLE staff, Tony met the others by the van and they boarded. Will took a seat on the middle bench and seemed to be lost in thought, a blessing to be sure.

Tony had no other choice than to sit next to him, by the door.

Linda sat in the front passenger seat. She whispered something to Garth and he started the van.

Tony leaned forward and stated the obvious. "Kat's not here yet."

Linda turned and smiled warmly. "She's staying behind to help the hands rub down the horses and get them settled for the night. One of the staff will give her a ride home when they're finished."

"Are you sure that's okay?" The question was out before he could stop it.

"Yes." She reached over the seat and patted his hand. "Kat will be fine. She needs time to sort things out, and horses have a calming influence on her."

"I hope you're right. I guess she worked in a stable in high school, so in a way it probably feels like home."

"Exactly."

Tony settled back in his seat and closed his eyes, pretending to doze off.

Will nudged him in the ribs with his elbow. "Kat was going to get me an ice pack for my ankle."

Opening one eye, Tony commented, "You're a big boy. Get your own ice pack."

"It's your fault. She stayed behind to avoid you."

Closing his eye, Tony ignored Sterling. But his words confirmed what Tony already suspected. He'd upset Kat badly enough that she was avoiding him. He hated to

think he'd hurt her. It was a precarious fence he strad-
dled between his duty to the Treadways and his desire
to keep Kat safe.

He had to be more cautious with Sterling. If the con
man got wind that someone was investigating him, he'd
go underground. Then where would Tony's case be? The
Treadways would be left with no resolution, and other
women like Lola and Kat would fall prey to Sterling's
cons. Tony couldn't let that happen.

Tomorrow he'd look for a chance to break into
Will's casita. He was done hoping the man would tip
his hand.

IT WAS WELL AFTER MIDNIGHT when George dropped
Kat off outside her casita. She waved goodbye as he
drove the battered ranch truck away, then she turned
to go inside.

A tall figure stepped out from the shadow of the
mesquite tree.

Her heart thudded heavily in her chest. She'd opened
her mouth to scream when a familiar male voice said,
"It's me. Tony."

"What are you doing here? You scared me."

"I wanted to make sure you were okay."

Kat couldn't meet his gaze, couldn't let him see how
much he'd affected her. She stepped onto the porch.
"Why wouldn't I be?"

"You were crying." He came over and cupped her
face with his hand. His touch was tender. "I'm sorry."

"Look, it's nothing. I'm fine."

"Has anyone told you you're a terrible liar?" he asked gently. "You can't even make eye contact."

She needed to run again. How was it that this man saw so easily what others couldn't? "Has anyone ever told you you're too damn observant?"

"Not recently. But it goes with the territory."

"As a security consultant?"

"Something like that." He rubbed her cheek with his thumb, a relatively innocent gesture that made her nerves come alive.

"Can we talk?" He sidestepped an Adirondack chair, crowding her.

She backed away, closer to the door. Right where she suspected he wanted her to be.

Stalling, she opted for a half-truth to distract him. "Okay, I was…emotional earlier. Being around the horses and you being…nice…brought up some old stuff."

"What kind of old stuff?" He nuzzled her ear, his breath warm and distracting.

"The usual teenage angst—wanting someone to care…wanting to feel needed—that kind of thing."

He stilled, then pulled back to look her in the eye. "It sounds like it might be more than that."

Oh, great, why had she thought this would be an effective stall? It was too damn revealing.

Protesting, she tried to pull away, but he held her by the shoulders. "Tell me, Kat."

She forced a laugh. "I didn't really have anything to angst about. My life was great. I did well in school, had two parents who loved me, and got to hang out in the stables with the horses. My dad was gone a lot, but that went along with his job as a district sales manager."

"So how does a girl with such a happy life end up thinking nobody wants or needs her?"

"I don't want to have this discussion. Go." She tried to jerk away from him, but his grip was firm.

"I'm not leaving, Kat. This is important."

Tossing her hair over her shoulder, she produced a seductive smile and hoped he couldn't feel the desperation oozing out her pores. She couldn't allow him to see the vulnerable teenage girl who still prompted her to make stupid mistakes.

She fell back on her most powerful weapon of distraction. Her body. Grasping his hand, she tugged him toward her door. "Talk is cheap. Why don't we go inside and get naked? That's what we both want, anyway."

He refused to budge.

"We talk here. Now."

Kat mustered all the righteous indignation she could manage. "Either you want me or you don't. Make up your mind. Because I'm done talking."

His smile was sad. "You can hate me all you want. And I'll probably hate myself tomorrow for passing on your offer. But…I care for you. And I'm not letting you off the hook, so you might as well open up. I can be very persistent, in case you haven't noticed."

"No shit." Running her hand through her hair, she paced a few steps away. "It's really a tired old story. My folks divorced when I was sixteen, and my world fell apart. They fought at times, but I thought that everybody did. Then one day I had to choose who I would live with."

She hesitated, afraid to look at him because she might see pity and that would destroy her composure. It annoyed her that the wound was still raw eighteen freaking years later. Suddenly wanting to get it all out on the table, she continued. "My younger sister went with Mom, and that meant Dad was all alone. I could see how lost he was, so I chose to live with him and take care of him. But he spent more and more time out of town on business. No matter how clean the house was, or how many dinners I learned to cook, he just... faded out of my life."

Searching Tony's expression, Kat saw concern. Compassion.

"He left you alone at sixteen?" His voice was husky, but there was no pity.

"While he was out of town. It wasn't his fault he had to make a living." The age-old instinct to defend her father rose up. "And he was home some weekends."

"Was he there for you when he was home?"

Kat hesitated. "As much as he could."

Tony was quiet for a moment, his expression unreadable in the dim porch light. "I had a...business partner once who could be in a room with me, but seem a million miles away. Like he was there, but not really there. Was it that way with your father?"

Kat nodded, not trusting herself to speak. It seemed so silly to feel abandoned and betrayed just because a parent didn't pay as much attention to her as she would have liked.

Raising her face, Kat said, "Yes, that's exactly what it was like. Most times he was behind closed doors, filing reports on his computer. Then there were a lot of evenings he'd be called out to an emergency meeting."

Tony traced her jaw, his touch warm and reassuring. "You were just a kid, a teen. All of the sudden the rug got pulled out from under you. And when you really needed your dad, he wasn't there for you. I can tell you one thing for sure. It wasn't because of anything you did or didn't do, or your worthiness. It was *his* problem. Got it?"

His understanding brought a lump to her throat. She wanted to believe him, but the little girl inside her who loved her daddy couldn't allow it.

"No, it had to have been something I'd done. Because otherwise…a father who cared wouldn't leave."

"Sometimes a parent can be too wrapped up in his own stuff to let his feelings show."

Kat absorbed his words, allowing the meaning to flow over her, filling in the cracks and crevices of her heart. To mend what had always seemed broken, though she couldn't really understand why.

"How do you know exactly what I need to hear?" Kat murmured, amazed at how good it felt to have someone tell her it wasn't her fault. She hadn't driven her dad away from home with her housekeeping or girlish chatter.

"Darlin', I'm just a dumb old Texan who every once in a while says something right."

She grasped his hand and kissed his callused palm, tenderness expanding in her chest. "Thank you."

He made a sound low in his throat. "My pleasure."

Dipping his head, he kissed her, and it was everything she'd imagined. He nibbled her lower lip, tracing it with his tongue until she parted her lips. His tongue swept inside.

Kat smiled against his mouth before she gave in to the sensations and textures of learning his kiss, his taste, his rhythm.

With a groan, he pulled back a few moments later. "What're you smiling about?"

"I knew you'd be a great kisser." With that, she looped her arms around his neck and tugged his head down for more.

His breath was uneven when he pulled away again. He closed his eyes, his jaw working. It seemed as if he was waging some sort of internal battle.

Finally, he opened his eyes and asked, "Is the offer still open?

Dazed, she tried to focus. "Offer?"

"To go inside…and get naked?"

Kat laughed, joy bubbling inside her. "Absolutely."

CHAPTER SEVENTEEN

TONY ABSORBED Kat's enthusiastic reply.

Absolutely, she wanted to get naked with him.

He didn't care that his professional ethics would be in tatters. He didn't care that he'd decided several hours ago to remain a detached observer.

Detachment wasn't possible after Kat started opening up to him. And when the offer of getting naked was dropped on the table, all thoughts of resisting were shot to hell.

But he also wanted to show her how much she meant to him. His chest literally ached at the thought that his feisty, funny Kat could have no idea how special she was. Or how wanted.

He intended to fix that immediately.

"Key card?" he murmured, before kissing her jaw. Nibbling lower, he was distracted by the pulse at her throat.

She whispered his name when he traced the sensitive spot with his tongue, then trailed wet kisses down her throat.

"Key card," he said again, more insistently.

"No." She shook her head.

"No what? No key?"

No, go away?

Kat laughed softly, reaching into her back pocket to remove her card. "I was trying to clear my head, something that's really hard to do with you kissing my throat like that."

Plucking it from her fingers, he turned to the door. He removed the card too quickly; the code flashed red.

"Damn."

He tried again, this time concentrating intently.

Green.

Grasping Kat by the hand, he propelled her into the room.

"You're sure you want this?" Tony felt duty bound to ask, though he didn't want a negative answer.

She stepped close and bracketed his face with her small, perfect hands, rubbing his stubbly cheek with her thumb. "I was in a bad place when I got back from the stables, and I desperately didn't want to be alone. And here you were. How did you know?"

"I didn't. I just knew *I* didn't want to be alone, and I needed to make things right with you."

"You're making things right by being here." Slowly, she unbuttoned her tailored shirt. The sight of her sliding the garment down her beautiful, pale arms made him wonder how he'd resisted this long. If the rest of her was half as stupendous as her delicate shoulders and full breasts caressed by a shimmery, peach-colored bra, he was a lucky, lucky man.

Any reservations he'd had were extinguished.

He was awed at the trust in her eyes and in her every gesture. All from a woman who didn't trust easily.

"Kat…" But what could he say? His instinct was to come clean and explain who he was, confess his real reason for being at Phoenix Rising.

"Shh." She unhooked her bra and let it slide to the floor.

He couldn't help but stare at the perfection of her breasts as she moved toward him, her delicate rose nipples inviting his touch, his tongue.

His jeans were growing uncomfortable as his erection pressed against the zipper. Letting out a growl of frustration, he shucked his own shirt and pulled her to him, relishing the soft curves pressed against his chest, where his heart pounded. Not only because she was gorgeous and smart, but because being with her, loving her, seemed right.

"I'm not who you think I am." The words slipped out without any conscious thought.

"It doesn't matter." Kat wrapped her arms around his waist and tipped her face up to be kissed, and he was a goner.

With a growl, Tony picked her up and gently placed her on the bed. Fortunately, he was past the age where he couldn't control his desire long enough for finesse, even when his body told him it wasn't necessary.

Her lips curved in a smile as he looked at her.

"I knew you'd be beautiful, but man, you are… gorgeous."

She raised her arms to him.

Scooping her against his chest, he was struck again with the rightness of being with her. And it wasn't simply because he'd gone without sex for several months. He'd had his share of women since his divorce, but none had touched him like this.

Kat challenged him, got inside his head. She trusted him with her secrets, an act of faith that both exhilarated and scared the shit out of him, making him wonder if he could measure up.

Tony vowed he would damn well try.

He kissed her eyes, her throat. Shifting lower, he swirled his tongue around one taut nipple, gratified when she moaned low in her throat. He grew harder in response.

Take it easy, Perez.

The pep talk didn't help. But visualizing his old boss dressed in drag did the trick almost too well.

Tony continued his exploration, loving the tastes and textures of Kat's body.

She arched her back as he dragged his tongue down to dip into her belly button, then lower. But denim impeded his progress.

"These have to go." He grinned, undoing the top button. She helped, tackling the zipper and wiggling free of the annoying garment.

Tony removed his jeans in near record time, but not before getting a condom from his wallet.

He needed to bury himself inside her, make her his

own. But he forced himself to put her first, plus drink his fill of her naked form. Well, almost naked. She still wore shimmery, peach-colored panties.

He trailed hot, wet kisses down her abdomen to the scrap of fabric, kissing lower still.

Her sharp intake of breath told him he'd found the right spot. Through the thin layer of lace, he caressed her with his tongue, sucking and nibbling until her spine arched and she called out his name, her hands clenching the comforter.

He let her savor the ripples of aftershock, then whispered, "These have to go, too." He slipped her underwear off and tangled his fingers in her red curls, savoring her hot slickness.

Kat pressed closer, reaching down to caress him. He thought he might explode right then and there.

Her mischievous chuckle told him that was exactly what she'd intended.

"Are you going to use this magnificent organ, or tease me all night?"

That was all the encouragement he needed.

He quickly tore open the condom packet and sheathed himself, then positioned himself above her, bracing on his elbows to look into her beautiful eyes. Then he kissed her deeply and plunged inside her. And gave himself over to sensation as they matched their movements.

When Kat wrapped her legs around his hips and gripped his shoulders, he welcomed release.

KAT STIRRED, unsure what had awakened her. It was dark outside and the bedside clock registered 3:00 a.m.

Deep, even breathing from the other side of the bed freaked her out. She froze, unable at first to place her companion.

Zach? God, please have it not mean she'd weakened and taken him back.

Then memories of Tony came flooding in, a kaleidoscope of passion and giving.

She rolled over so she could look at him.

His jaw was shadowed, his hair mussed, dipping low on his forehead. She ached to smooth it back, but didn't want to wake him. She needed this time to gain her equilibrium before she faced the morning-after awkwardness, which could arrive any time between now and when the maid knocked on the door to clean.

Sighing, Kat refused to regret bringing Tony into her bed. She had needed someone, anyone, when she returned last night.

But that wasn't true. It was only Tony who seemed able to see past her bravado and understand how terribly lonely she'd been. Tony had been there for her when she'd needed him the most.

But what had he meant when he'd said he wasn't who she thought he was? At the time, she hadn't cared, but now she had to wonder....

He stirred, saying her name in his sleep. What woman wouldn't love knowing she was deep in a man's subconscious even when he slept?

Zach had called out other women's names more than

once. Kat had convinced herself they were previous girlfriends, but she now thought they might have been more current. He'd lied about so many things, why would monogamy be any different?

There was a dull ache at the thought of Zach being unfaithful, but not the pain she would have felt a month ago.

As she watched Tony, he opened his eyes, a question in the golden depths.

"Hey." He reached out and smoothed her forehead with his fingertips. "No frowning after you make love with me. It might hurt my fragile ego."

She laughed, no longer afraid of morning-after awkwardness. Not with him.

"You have many faults, but a fragile ego is not one of them."

"Ouch, you hurt my feelings." His grin said otherwise.

What a startling contrast to Zach, who had needed to be assured on a regular basis that he was the best she'd ever had. It had become an empty ritual, as empty as their relationship.

Placing her palms on either side of Tony's jaw, she kissed him lightly.

He deepened the kiss. And she felt his erection pressing against her belly.

Caressing his muscular calf with her foot, she threw her leg over his to draw him to her. She wanted to hold him close and never let him go.

"I like the way you think." He rolled onto his back, pulling her on top, kissing her hungrily.

Straddling him, she moved her hips, rocking against his hardness. "Ahh."

He grasped her arms and stilled her movement. She tried to wriggle out of his grasp, a maneuver that made him groan as if in pain.

"You're killing me here," he muttered.

"What's the problem?" She was slightly irritated that he was tarnishing her early morning glow.

"I didn't plan this. I brought only one condom. So unless you…"

Kat grinned wickedly, shifting so that she was poised above his tip. Nuzzling his ear, she whispered, "You'd really say no to me?"

"No?" It came out sounding like a plea.

Kat widened her eyes innocently. "So how much would a condom be worth to you right now?"

"Right now, darlin'? Priceless."

"Why?"

He groaned. "Because making love with you is *that* phenomenal."

"In that case, I think I can accommodate you." She rolled to the side, taking one long, lingering look over her shoulder at his muscled torso and obvious enthusiasm.

Hurrying to the closet, she got a box out of her suitcase.

She returned to the bed, resumed the delightful position she'd been in before he'd interrupted, and dumped twelve condoms on his chest. "Think that'll be enough?"

He threw back his head and laughed. "I think I love you, Kat."

Her glow dimmed slightly at his joking use of the endearment when she longed to hear those three words spoken sincerely and without reserve. But she ignored the tiny seed of sadness trying to take root in her heart. Tony wasn't the kind of man to love her, despite her protests that she was worthy. He might want her, but he didn't need her in the all-consuming way Zach had. She had always known Zach wouldn't leave, because he needed her to keep his world rotating. And that was where her security had taken root. She would never have that reassurance with Tony, because he was plenty capable himself.

But as long as she knew where she stood, she wouldn't get hurt, Kat told herself. Ripping open a packet, she placed the contents in his palm while she leaned forward to kiss him deeply, her tongue matching the motion of her hips, letting him know exactly what she wanted.

He sheathed himself, grasping her hips to thrust inside her. His eyes closed as he let out a sigh.

One lone tear escaped down her cheek.

CHAPTER EIGHTEEN

TONY LAY AWAKE, staring up at the ceiling long after Kat's breathing had slowed and she'd drifted off to sleep. His body felt energized after a night of lovemaking, ready to take on the world.

His mind, on the other hand, went around in frustrating circles. Was he in love with Kat? Even with morning-after perspective he didn't have a clue.

What had he been thinking, sleeping with a woman intricately involved in his case? Nobody close to him would excuse what he'd done. Not his old partner from the Rangers, Ryan, or his mother, who could still flatten him merely by saying his middle name and giving him "the look."

Both would tell him that what he'd done was dangerous on a personal and professional level. His mother would insist a relationship founded on lies didn't stand a chance. She'd deliver a smack to the back of his head to punctuate her point that Kat was much too nice a girl to be treated this way. Then tell him she'd raised him better. And his two younger brothers, Christian and Paul, would never let him hear the end of it.

But he finally surrendered to sleep….

A knock at the door made Tony and Kat start. He watched her jump up and throw on her robe.

The second knock was more insistent, rattling the door on its hinges.

"Kat? Are you all right?" It was Will.

She glanced at Tony, pleading with her eyes. It was obvious she wanted him to make himself scarce.

He raised an eyebrow, but didn't move. Tony Perez didn't hide from anyone. But he didn't sleep with a woman peripherally involved in his case, either. If Will knew he'd slept with Kat, all bets were off.

Sighing, Tony threw back the covers and grabbed his clothes, hoping Kat could get rid of the guy quickly. It was a new experience for Tony to run away after making love with a woman. It wasn't pleasant.

Once he was beyond the line of sight and headed toward the bathroom, she opened the door a crack, tightening the belt of her robe.

Tony stood in the bathroom entryway and listened.

"You weren't at breakfast this morning. I was worried, so I thought I'd check on my way to the gym. Brooke offered to ice down my ankle."

Kat cleared her throat. "I, um, overslept. I was up late last night."

"What time did you get back from the stables? I didn't hear a vehicle."

The man must sleep like the dead if he hadn't heard the old ranch truck.

"It was after midnight."

"I should have waited up for you."

Will's presence might have prevented Tony from a night of sex with Kat. How could such a satisfying night be destructive on so many levels?

Kat tightened her belt again. "No need. I'm a big girl and I can handle myself."

"Don't you ever want a little help…someone to help you handle things?"

Kat didn't cut Will off at the knees as Tony expected. Instead, she said, "I left the shower running—I'd better go. But I really appreciate you stopping by."

Her appreciation was wasted. Will was about as genuinely considerate as Benedict Arnold.

"Save me a place at lunch?" Sterling practically begged.

Tony hoped Kat would tell Will she couldn't see him anymore. Then his conscience pricked, because he knew he couldn't continue a relationship with her. He hated to think of the hurt he would cause her, but ending this now was the honorable thing to do. The *only* thing to do. Plus, he still might be able to salvage his investigation.

"Sure. I'll see you then."

"What?" He must have misunderstood what he'd just heard her say.

"Why don't you throw on your suit under your clothes," Will suggested, "and we can lounge around the pool? Have a few drinks, take it easy."

"Um, sure. It's a beautiful day for a swim. I'll save you a place at lunch."

Tony jerked on his boxers and his jeans, relishing the

harsh noise the zipper made. It would serve her right if Sterling figured out she had a man in her room.

Kat threw a panicked look over her shoulder, then said loudly, "I'll see you then, Will. Bye."

Stepping into the bathroom, Tony closed the door behind him. He braced his hands against the sink and shut his eyes. How had he let things get so out of hand? And why did it feel as if she had betrayed him, when he was about to end things with her?

He forced himself to remember his responsibility to his client, pushing down his hurt and confusion. This would give him an easy out with Kat. One thing was for sure, he would *never* make this mistake again.

When Tony emerged from the bathroom, dressed and ready to leave, he was back on track.

Kat moved toward him. She gave him that slow, seductive smile that made his heart lurch. "I was hoping we would shower together."

He tipped her chin up with his hand. "I don't share well. And it looks like your dance card is filling up, darlin'."

"Tony, it's not—"

He stopped her, placing his finger on her lips. "It is. But that's okay. No harm, no foul. I wasn't in it for keeps, anyway."

He turned and walked out the door.

WILL LEANED BACK in his lounge chair, sipping his Gray Goose martini as he watched Kat remove her shorts and T-shirt, fold them and stow them in her straw bag.

Her white bikini revealed an expanse of creamy skin. You could hardly even see she had some freckles. Her curves were truly inspiring. Overall, she was quite delectable.

Smiling, he closed his eyes. This might be his best job ever. And if she was very, very lucky, he might decide on a more permanent arrangement. Having a wife with a reputation of being honest and reliable could come in handy in so many instances. He envisioned a home with a picket fence, kids and a dog. The perfect front.

A few minutes later Kat rolled onto her stomach, giving him the opportunity to set his seduction in motion.

"Would you like me to rub some lotion on your back? You don't want to get burned." He infused his voice with the right amount of concern.

"I'm...fine."

He let it go for the time being. They chatted about the weather and Will's work.

"Your shoulders are getting pink." He rose before she could protest, grabbing her bottle of lotion. His hands fairly itched to touch her firm, young flesh.

Slathering the cream on Kat's back, he enjoyed the way his hands glided over her back. He kneaded her neck and shoulders. "You're so tense. It must be all that stable work yesterday."

"Mmm-hmm."

He intended to wait until the sun and alcohol did

their work, and then he'd suggest they go back to his suite, where he'd help her really relax.

TONY SAT ON THE PATIO at the café, sipping his Corona and watching Kat and Will at the pool below.

Jealousy burned in his gut.

When Will parked his butt on Kat's lounge chair and started rubbing sunblock on her shoulders, Tony thought he might jump over the railing.

And since he was two stories up, that would have been a bad idea for more than professional reasons.

Even this far off, it wasn't hard to decipher Will's agenda. The way he touched Kat every chance he got, the predatory way he eyed her from behind his sunglasses, all spoke of a man with scoring on his mind.

Tony wanted to make him sorry he'd ever glanced at Kat. He wanted to tell her the guy was a slimeball. Wait. He'd already warned her. But for her to believe him, he'd have to admit why he was here. And put his self-respect on the line.

The job came first. He'd given up his career for a woman once and didn't intend to do it again. Besides, Kat seemed content to move from one man to the next.

Tony pushed aside his gut instinct that she wasn't interested in sleeping with Will. Chances were good that she'd been caught off guard and had simply been too nice to say no to the man's invitation. But making allowances for her behavior did not help Tony's resolve, so he quickly discarded the idea.

Instead, he decided this would be the perfect opportunity to search Will's casita. The man looked like he would be otherwise occupied for another half hour at the very least.

Of course, if he was being honest, Tony would have to admit there was a slim possibility he was running away from Kat because he was a coward. He'd failed miserably in his marriage. Hell, he'd had no idea Corrine was unhappy until she'd told him they had an appointment with a marriage counselor. Then, when all her hurt and anger came pouring out, he'd felt as if he'd been sucker punched. He'd had no freaking clue. So why would he think he could do any better with Kat, a woman who didn't begin to know who he really was?

Rubbing his jaw, Tony decided sometimes a touch of cowardice was a good thing.

Survival instincts and all.

THE SUN'S RAYS ON her back felt wonderful, and Kat relaxed, avoiding thinking about Tony. Of course, the martini Will ordered for her hadn't hurt.

They had the pool area to themselves, the lush tropical plants a marked contrast to the high desert grounds beyond the wrought-iron fence. The rock waterfall recirculated water, its hypnotic trickling reminding Kat of one of those white noise machines that were supposed to help people sleep.

Stifling a yawn, she had to admit it certainly worked. A nap beckoned.

"This is great." Will seemed more laid-back than

usual. The two martinis he'd had in such a short time might have something to do with it.

"Mmm."

She may have dozed for a minute or two before his voice broke the silence again.

"Tell me what it's like winning a lottery."

Kat repressed a sigh. Quiet would have been nice. But then, she was short-tempered from her exhausting night, and he was simply trying to make conversation. It wasn't his fault she'd slept with Tony and then gotten all confused, agreeing to a lunch date with Will.

Devastation didn't come close to what she'd felt when she understood Tony thought the worst of her, and had so easily cast her aside. Apparently making love hadn't been as special for him as it had been for her. They'd connected in an amazing way that had convinced her she was in over her head; possibly past the point of no return. Kat had put her heart and soul into every moment of lovemaking last night.

She ached to curl up in a ball now and have a good cry. Or call her friend Annie and rake Tony over the coals. Annie could always make her feel better.

"Kat? You didn't answer my question."

Rolling over, she pulled her sunglasses down over her eyes to hide her emotions. "What...? Oh, the lottery. I was, um, shocked. And excited, then scared."

"Why scared?"

"Because I've never had that much money at one time and I was afraid I'd screw up and lose it all."

There was no way she would admit she'd felt some-how...unworthy...of such a windfall.

He reached over and grasped her hand, threading his fingers through hers. His gaze was lazy and...attentive. "I'm surprised you don't have a financial advisor."

"I'm a CPA. I don't need an advisor."

"What's the saying? An accountant who handles his own investments has a fool for a client?"

Kat disengaged her hand, reaching for her drink. "I think that's for attorneys and doctors."

"Still sound advice."

"Yes, I imagine it is." She sipped her martini, but it did nothing to chase away her angst.

What the hell, she thought, and drained the rest.

"You invested in the stock market?"

The personal question made her uncomfortable, even though the vodka started to make her feel warm and fuzzy. But it would take more than a martini for her to disclose her finances to someone she didn't know well. "A bit."

"That's good. Diversification is important."

"Mmm-hmm." Kat reclined the lounge chair, removed her sunglasses and closed her eyes.

Will was blessedly silent.

Her thoughts drifted back to the night she'd spent with Tony and how right it had seemed to be with him. How she'd shared information with him she'd never told another man, and he'd been...reassuring. Until he'd closed her out. Without giving her the chance to apologize.

"You were smiling a few minutes ago."

She cranked open one eye, tamping down her irritation. "I'm…enjoying my vacation. I needed one. I didn't realize how much until I got here."

"You work a lot?"

She nodded. "Sixty hours a week, usually."

Especially when she'd needed every penny to pay her own bills and a good portion of Zach's, as well. And bailing him out of jail twice hadn't been cheap, either, along with attorney's fees to defend him in the two DUI cases. He'd had the bad luck to get stopped the few times he'd been out drinking. Or so he'd said.

Kat had bought the explanation at the time, but now it seemed plain naive. Thirty-year-old men should be smart enough not to drink and drive in the first place.

"I'd never want to impose on our…friendship, but as a life coach, I help clients achieve financial health."

Opening her eyes, Kat turned her head to look at him. "Really? I thought it was more helping with career paths and things of that nature."

"Financial well-being is the baseline. In Maslow's hierarchy of needs, food and shelter come first before someone can even think of the higher levels of love, acceptance, etc."

Kat only vaguely recalled the mention of Maslow in her Psych 101 course, and couldn't begin to converse on the subject. "That sounds logical," she murmured.

"I have quite a reputation in my field and I'm paid

well for my services. But I've been known to advise friends for free. It's the least I can do." His smile was eager, open. "I'd be happy to help you, Kat."

"That's…very nice." She shifted uncomfortably.

"I have my laptop back in my room. We'll take a look at your portfolios and I can give you a second opinion. Think of me as a backup of sorts."

Moving her chair to the upright position, Kat put on her sunglasses. "I'm grateful that you want to help, Will. But I'm not comfortable with that."

"Oh." Hurt flashed in his eyes and she felt as if she'd kicked a puppy. "Not a problem. Just thought I'd offer."

"Thank you. Really."

"You're welcome."

But Kat could tell she'd wounded his ego. He became very quiet.

She hated when she disappointed people.

"It's a beautiful day. This was a great idea," she enthused. "Thank you for inviting me."

"A beautiful day and a beautiful woman." He smiled broadly, but she could tell he was still sad.

Her urge to cheer him up was strong, but not strong enough to give him access to her financial information.

She was searching to change the topic when Tony entered the pool area. He placed a glass on one of the round tables on the other side of the pool and sat under an umbrella.

Designer sunglasses shaded his eyes, but she knew darn well he'd seen them. She suspected he was spying on them. He had a lot of nerve, after practically running from her suite this morning. What had he said? "No harm, no foul."

Leaning back in his seat, he sipped his drink. Then waved, as if he'd just noticed them.

Kat return his wave, when she really wanted to give him the one-finger salute.

Will ignored him completely.

She couldn't help but notice how great Tony looked in his navy-blue swim trunks. His chest was a bronze expanse of muscles that tapered down to a very respectable six-pack. Her cheeks warmed as she recalled trailing kisses down his abs and, later, wrapping her legs around his lean hips.

Glancing sideways at Will, she realized he'd never removed his Tommy Bahama shirt. Somehow she suspected he had love handles hidden beneath the flowing palm trees. But the really telling piece of information was she hadn't noticed until now that he hadn't taken off his shirt. Or been even the slightest bit intrigued by what lay beneath.

No doubt about it. Good guys just didn't do it for her.

A shadow fell across her and Kat was almost afraid to look up.

Finally, she turned her head and allowed her gaze to scan Tony's familiar form, coming to rest on his face.

No doubt about it. He did it for her. And how.

But last night, Tony hadn't seemed dangerous or devastating.

He'd simply seemed right.

CHAPTER NINETEEN

TONY STOOD AT THE FOOT of Kat's chaise lounge, wanting to throw her across his shoulder and carry her away. This was a new reaction for him.

He was closer to nailing Sterling now that he'd searched his suite. It had been clean—too clean. There had been absolutely nothing personal in it. And then, Tony had discovered the false bottom in Will's can of shaving cream. Simplistic, but effective.

"Hello, Kat." He nodded tightly to Will. "Sterling."

Will returned his nod. "You seem to be turning up everywhere, Tony."

"Yeah, I'm good at that."

He waited for Kat to say something, anything.

But she didn't.

"I need a word with you."

She stared up at him, her expression unreadable behind the sunglasses.

"I'm sure it can wait until later." Her voice was cool, impersonal.

He was tempted to say he'd left his boxers in her room last night, but thought better of it. For now. Instead, he nudged a lounge chair closer to hers with his foot and settled in.

"Beautiful day," he commented.

"What are you doing?" Her tone was still frigid.

"Getting some sun, just like you."

Lowering her head, she stared at him over the top of her sunglasses. Her pinched expression was that of a librarian at the beach. And he suspected she had some sand rubbing her the wrong way. "We didn't invite you to join us."

"I don't need an invitation. I'm a paying guest, like you."

"Kat, is there something I should know?" Will eyed Tony suspiciously.

"Nothing." She pushed her glasses up. "Tony is just irritated that I rebuffed his overtures this morning. He's a sore loser."

Her lie would be laughable if it didn't make him feel achy and forlorn, like a kid alone with the flu. He hadn't felt this way since he'd come home from a double shift to find Corrine had moved out all her stuff.

Will leaned close and draped his arm around Kat's shoulders, caressing her bare skin with his fingers. "I can hardly fault him for finding you irresistible. Any red-blooded man would. But as the saying goes, two's company, three's a crowd, Tony. Why don't you leave us alone."

The man's possessiveness set Tony's blood boiling. Criminals tended to escalate their behavior. What if Sterling had become physically violent since he'd manipulated Eunice Treadway?

"I'll leave," Tony said, "if Kat agrees to meet me later."

"I don't think so." Her response was tart.

He reclined the chair, crossing his arms behind his head. "Suit yourself. I've got all day."

Five minutes later, she capitulated. "I'll meet you at the hummingbird garden at four o'clock."

Smiling, Tony rose from the lounge chair. "See you then." He whistled as he sauntered away.

Only he didn't feel nearly as confident as he tried to appear. He couldn't stand by and let Kat put herself at risk. And he had the feeling he couldn't just walk away from what they'd shared, either.

But he could hardly tell her what he knew about Sterling. There was no doubt she would let something slip, putting herself in greater danger, or prompting Sterling to go into hiding.

Tony would have to think of something and quick. Hopefully, he could decipher the coded spreadsheet he'd downloaded from the flash drive in Sterling's shaving cream can. At least he had a place to start.

KAT PUT THE FINISHING touches on her hair. She'd softened the natural curls with styling gel, but there were still ringlets galore. The cream-colored slacks flattered her rear end; the peach halter top set off the slight suntan from this afternoon. And her cleavage was very much front and center.

She was dressed to seduce.

Not that she intended to seduce Will, but she wouldn't mind if Tony got that impression. High schoolish? Definitely. But the man had practically bolted from her room after making love to her all night. And given his stamp of approval on her date with Will.

No harm, no foul. They'd see about that.

Checking her makeup one more time, she grabbed her purse and left, making sure her door locked behind her.

The hummingbird garden was tucked away near the café and front entrance. It was public, but not a lot of people went there. She'd discovered it recently and loved the solitude, as well as watching hummingbirds flit from flower to flower. Yellow and orange butterflies were an occasional bonus.

Glancing at her watch, she saw she was a few minutes early. For some reason, she'd hoped Tony would be here early, too. Maybe she wanted to believe he could hardly wait to see her. Or had reconsidered and wanted to tell her she meant the world to him and he couldn't live without her. It scared her how badly she wanted him.

How stupid. Here she was, thinking he'd discovered she was indispensible after an evening of lovemaking with her. Talk about fairy tales.

A low whistling behind her alerted her to Tony's presence as he walked into the garden.

She turned, suddenly feeling unsure of herself.

He didn't move, just stood there and stared at her.

See anything you like?

No, that sounded too cliché. And desperate.

Kat raised her chin. "You wanted to talk to me."

"Um, yeah. You look spectacular."

"Thank you." She moved to a stone bench, brushed it off with her hand and sat.

Tony sat next to her. Not close enough to touch, though, dammit.

His usual scent combined with coconut suntan lotion enveloped her. She wanted to lean her head on his shoulder and absorb it. But of course she didn't. Her pride demanded that he remain unaware of how pathetically in love with him she was.

The thought made her freeze. She'd done it again. She'd fallen for a man who was incapable of giving her the white picket fence. What's more, he didn't want her except for a night's diversion. At least Zach had wanted her for a lot more than that. What if he'd been the best she could do?

She tried to put that awful idea right out of her mind. Her voice was cool when she asked, "What is it?"

Good, no trace of vulnerability.

"You need to be careful with Sterling. He's not what you think."

She raised her chin. "That same tired story. What is he then?"

"I can't tell you. Just take my word."

"And I should listen to you because…? Let me guess, because you're so honest and straightforward in your dealings with me? We shared some pretty spectacular moments last night, but this morning you wouldn't give me the chance to explain why I agreed to meet Will. I didn't mean to follow through…. But I wasn't able to tell him right there, face-to-face, when my emotions were all over the place…after making love with you."

Clearing his throat, he moved closer. But still not close enough to touch. "You have to believe me, Kat. I think you're a wonderful woman and…if things were different…there's nothing that would keep me away from you. *Nothing.*"

His ambiguities made her angry. He was very adept at saying everything and nothing at all. "If what things were different?"

He glanced away. "Great use of xeriscape."

"Yes, the plaque over there—" she pointed to a bronze rectangle near the footpath "—says they're all native plants that require little water. As if you *care.* Now, are you going to answer my question?"

"I can't."

"Can't or won't?"

He shifted, squaring his jaw. "I won't."

"Then there's nothing more for us to talk about."

Kat's chest ached as she stood to leave. Still, she hoped he'd stop her. Hoped he'd open up and tell the truth.

But he remained on the bench as she took the footpath back the way she had come.

LOOKING THROUGH THE white wood blinds, Will saw Kat dash to her casita and let herself in.

His search of her room had been quick, efficient and fruitless. She hadn't brought any hard-copy organizers or files with her, and he hadn't been able to get past the password prompt on her laptop. As an accountant, she was probably more savvy about computer security than most.

No matter. He had an excellent contingency plan. Sex with Kat was the next and very pleasurable step to bind her to him and gain her trust. And truth be told, he was impatient for it. He'd awakened rock hard this morning after dreaming of how special he would make her feel, how many ways he would pleasure her as they consummated their relationship. After that, she'd beg to marry him. All that was hers would become his. Including her health insurance, paycheck and condo in Tempe—on top of her lottery proceeds. And then they'd make two or three beautiful babies to further lull his clients into trusting him.

Yes, Kat Monroe could very well be his most brilliant endeavor yet. Small potatoes in the short term, but solid gold long term.

CHAPTER TWENTY

TONY WAS DRAWN TO the art studio by some instinct he couldn't understand. Probably because he worked with his hands when he had a lot on his mind. And when he'd been with the Rangers, he could always swing by one of the usual hangouts and find someone he trusted as a sounding board. Garth seemed like a pretty down-to-earth guy, despite being an artist.

The studio itself was locked, but Tony heard the sweet clang of metal on metal coming from the shop. Taking the path around back, he was greeted by the aroma of hot iron.

Garth was wearing huge leather gloves and a welding hood. Tony watched him heat a metal tube in the kiln, then pound on it when it was cool enough to shape. He used a handheld torch to heat certain areas and then twist or curve the iron as needed. Then, sparks flying, he welded pieces together.

Not wanting to startle the artist, Tony walked within his line of sight, careful not to focus on the dazzling sparks without protective eye gear.

Garth stopped, flipping up the hood. "Hey."

"Hey. Wrought-iron?"

"Yeah. I switch mediums every once in a while. It challenges me and frees up my creativity. I got a killer deal on this old kiln and thought I'd give iron a try. Can I do something for you?"

"Let me hang out for a while? Let me clean your shop. Anything to keep my hands busy and clear my head."

Garth nodded. "No problem. Push broom's over in that closet. Ever work with iron?"

"Nah. Just a few projects around the house. My welds are sloppy."

"Yeah, mine, too." He grinned. "But it's a hell of a lot of fun. Maybe when you get done sweeping, you can give it a try. You can't be any worse than I am."

"You've got a deal." Tony's mood was lighter already. Some problems just couldn't be solved without dirt, sweat and swearing.

Tony hummed as he swept; he was more than a little disturbed to realize the tune was "I Love the Way You Love Me" by John Michael Montgomery. He put a lid on the humming after that.

Once he'd disposed of all the debris, he noticed a stain on the concrete. A cabinet marked Cleaning Supplies yielded rags and solvent. Cloth in hand, he applied elbow grease to the spot.

Now this was satisfying.

Not nearly as satisfying as having Kat's body writhing beneath him in bed, but the fallout was certainly much simpler. Stained concrete he could understand. Women, not so much.

It frustrated him that she wouldn't simply take his word that Sterling was dangerous. She'd trusted him enough to sleep with him, but not enough to heed his warning. What was up with that?

But then again, she'd made a date with Will right after sleeping with Tony, too. They hadn't gotten far with *that* issue in their terse conversation in the garden.

"You're going to rub a hole right through that concrete if you keep it up." Garth stood watching him, arms folded over his chest. "Only a woman could cause that kind of frustration."

Tony grunted and continued to work on the stain.

"Care to bang on some metal?"

Conceding defeat, he rose. "Yeah."

He followed Garth to the workbench. Nodding toward the mangled pieces of iron, he asked, "What're you trying to accomplish?"

Garth wiped his face on his shirtsleeve. "That's what's so great. I'm not trying to accomplish anything. I get to play when I learn a new technique or medium. So mostly I'm just heating, getting a feel for variables and the changes in the metal. Trying different techniques. I give myself permission to play like a kid at this stage."

Tony raised his eyebrow. "Cool. I think I'd like being an artist."

"Yeah, I'm fortunate. But it's work, too—not all fun and games."

"I guess that's the same with most jobs."

Garth selected a long section of iron pipe and handed it to Tony. "There, pound on that with the hammer as hard as you can."

Tony complied, gaining fierce enjoyment from whaling on the pipe. As hard as he hit it with the hammer, he couldn't manage more than a couple small dings.

"Women are a lot like iron. You don't get a true idea of their beauty until life heats up."

"Spare me the lecture," Tony growled.

Garth raised his hands in defeat. "Just trying to help, man."

KAT WENT BACK TO HER suite after her argument with Tony. It was a good thing Will wouldn't be there to take her to dinner until six, because her emotions were all over the place. Her one clear thought was that she couldn't continue to see Will. It wasn't fair to him, when she was tied up in knots over another man. A man who seemed to be every bit as bad a choice as Zach had been.

Giving Will the news after dinner would be hard. She hated to hurt his feelings. And hated admitting to herself she wasn't attracted to him. She'd tried, really tried to give him a chance. But next to Tony he seemed like half a man.

And Tony wasn't interested in a relationship with her or, apparently, in telling the truth. She'd initially blamed herself that she'd gotten flustered and accepted Will's invitation to lunch. But Tony hadn't wanted to listen to her explanation this morning or this afternoon.

He'd made up his mind. Maybe he'd always seen her as just one-night-stand material. Because men like Tony didn't need a woman like Kat to buffer life for them—they could handle it on their own.

And when it was all said and done, wasn't that what Kat had to offer? A nice, safe place to land when the reality of being an adult got too tedious?

Biting her lip, she willed the tears away. She would *not* cry over one more failure with men.

Her cell phone rang and she groaned when she saw it was her mother. Kat could not handle another in-depth description of Nicole's most recent ob-gyn visit.... But what if something was wrong?

She flipped open her phone. "Hi, Mom, what's up? Is Nicole okay?"

"She's fine, dear. Uncomfortable, grumpy and ready for the baby to arrive, but fine. I'm calling about your e-mail."

Kat had to stop and think. "Oh, yeah, when I asked you and Sharon about Dad."

"I talked to Sharon…and there's a reason your father has been…unavailable."

Kat wasn't surprised her mom and Sharon kept in touch. They had a remarkably civilized relationship. But her dad being out of contact with Sharon was not a good thing.

"Don't tell me they split up."

"Oh, no, nothing like that. Something has come up that would be best discussed directly with your father.

Sharon says he wants to talk to you, but right now e-mail would be best. He'll be in touch."

"Explaining what? I knew something had to be really wrong." Panic started to overtake Kat as she considered the worst-case scenario. "Is he dying?"

"No, he is definitely *not* dying."

"Why won't you tell me what's wrong then?"

"Because it's not my information to share. Don't worry. He'll explain. Now, I have to go. Nicole says she's having back pain and we need to call the doctor. I'll call again soon."

Kat clicked her phone shut, exhaling slowly.

If her father was able to explain, then it wasn't life threatening. She needn't jump to conclusions or freak out. Everything would be fine.

Pulling her laptop out of the case, she was interrupted by a knock at the door.

"Come on in," she said, after swinging it open.

Will's face was pale, his mouth taut with pain. He leaned heavily on his crutches.

"What happened?" She rushed to his side. "You were doing so much better."

"I was feeling so much better that I went for a walk after I dropped you off here. The path was uneven and I must've stepped wrong."

"Come in and sit down. I just have to check my e-mail for a sec."

"We don't have time. Garth is busy with the golf cart, so we'll have to walk. As slow as I am with these things, we'll be lucky to make dinner."

"It'll only take a minute—"

"I'm not sure how long I can wait. I've been holding off taking a pain pill because I didn't want to spoil our evening."

Kat experienced a stab of irritation, followed by remorse for being so cold and heartless. He was in pain, yet his first thought was of their plans.

Taking one longing glance at her laptop, she grabbed her purse.

TONY SAT IN THE CORNER of the dining room and watched Linda wend her way among the tables, stopping to speak at each one. She was just as friendly and gracious talking to Will as to anyone else. Since Lorraine and Lola had joined Kat and Will, she spent extra time at their table.

Could she and Garth be supplying Will with information on possible marks? His gut told him no. But she might have information about him.

He'd chosen to sit alone at a small table, and had eaten his dinner quickly so he could have a word with Linda when he was done.

Finally, she worked her way to his corner.

"Tony, what are you doing here all by yourself? I think there's a space at the table with Kat and the others." She put extra emphasis on Kat's name, as if she'd noticed his growing attraction to her.

"Actually, I was hoping I might talk to you for a few minutes."

"Of course." She pulled out the chair next to him and sat. "What can I do for you?"

"You seem intuitive about your guests, and I understand a lot of them are repeat customers."

"Yes, we're very proud of our repeat business. Word of mouth is the best advertising."

"I can certainly see why Phoenix Rising has such a stellar reputation."

The waiter came by and poured coffee for Tony. He glanced at Linda, but she shook her head.

"What can you tell me about Will Sterling?"

She tilted her chin. "This is his first visit with us and I've found him to be very...personable."

"How was he referred to you?"

Linda cleared her throat. "We have a policy of confidentiality."

"I wouldn't ask if it wasn't important. I'm concerned that he might not be what he seems. You certainly wouldn't want someone preying on your more vulnerable guests."

Her shock was genuine. "Absolutely not."

"So do you think you might be able to speak in hypotheticals with me?"

"You're law enforcement, aren't you?"

"Retired." He didn't want to reveal his reason for being there, but didn't see that he had a choice. "I'm now a security consultant. Hypothetically, a man may have struck up a friendship with my client's mother... and taken advantage of the elderly woman."

"Will Sterling?"

Tony nodded. He tried to be tactful with the next question, but there was no easy way of saying it. "Is there anyone in your employ you think might tip him off about wealthy, single women due to arrive?"

"No. All of our employees have been here since we opened five years ago. They're local and I would have heard if any were less than honest."

"I'm sorry, I had to ask."

"I understand."

"Who referred Sterling?"

Linda frowned. "If I remember correctly, it was a travel agent."

"Did the same travel agent book anyone else who's staying here now?"

"I'll have to double check my records…."

"Kat?"

"No, a friend of mine, June Marsh, referred Kat." Linda hesitated. "Let me think a minute."

"Lorraine and Lola?"

She snapped her fingers. "That's it."

"I'll need the name and address of the travel agency, along with the booking agent's name."

"Of course. I'll get the information tonight." The innkeeper's eyes grew shadowed. "I'd hate it if someone used our resort like that, but I will help you any way I can."

"Thanks, Linda." He squeezed her hand. "I need you to keep this quiet. And please don't change your behavior in the least."

The back of his neck prickled and he glanced up

to find Kat staring at him from across the room. She quickly looked away.

"Of course." Linda followed the direction of his gaze. "You don't think she's in danger, do you?"

"I'll make sure she's safe."

CHAPTER TWENTY-ONE

KAT WAITED OUTSIDE Will's door, holding his crutches while he inserted the key card. She'd managed to make it through the interminable dinner, made slightly less excruciating by Lola and Lorraine's presence.

A tension headache gripped her temples and all she wanted to do was crawl into bed, alone, and forget this day ever happened. Or even better, check her e-mail and find out that her father was fine, deeply apologetic over worrying her, and determined to bridge the gulf between them.

But she'd realized during dinner that Will would need help getting back to his room. She'd delayed her speech to let him down easily, and here they were.

"You'll come in for a drink, won't you?" He opened the door with a flourish, a gesture that was seemed out of place considering he was balancing himself on one leg.

"Will, we need to talk."

"We can talk inside."

"What I have to say can be said out here."

He nodded. "All right. But my leg is starting to throb…

and I feel like a flamingo." His chuckle was forced, as if he sensed this wasn't going to be pleasant news.

"Here." She handed him his crutches. And felt crummy. How could she dump him like this?

Clearing his throat, he said, "I appreciated your help tonight. I've never met a kinder woman. Your friendship means so much to me."

That made her feel even worse.

Will shifted, wincing in pain. "I'm sorry, I have to get off my ankle." Propping the crutches under his arm, he turned to go inside, catching a crutch on the door frame and stumbling.

Kat caught her breath as he swayed. "Here, let me help you." Taking the crutch from him, she placed his arm on her shoulders and wrapped hers around his waist.

"Thank you," he said, leaning heavily on her. The weight of his arm made her feel trapped. She forced herself to take a deep breath and do what needed to be done.

Fortunately, there was a light on in the room and she steered him toward an easy chair. He sat, closing his eyes against the pain.

"Can I get you your medicine? A glass of water?"

Will opened his eyes. "No, I'll…manage. You've been an absolute angel. I don't know what I would have done without you."

This time his compliment soothed her wounded spirit.

She *was* a good person. Needed and helpful. Not

the kind of woman who should be tossed aside like so much garbage.

"I'm happy to help."

"I'm hesitant to impose on our friendship, but I have a favor to ask. If it's too much, please just tell me and I'll make other arrangements."

"What is it?"

"I was able to get a doctor's appointment tomorrow afternoon in Jasper. I'd ask Garth to drive me, but he's so busy with his artwork—he's putting on another show for guests at one and…" He looked away.

Kat touched his shoulder, wishing she could be the woman he wanted her to be. "Of course I'll take you."

He met her gaze and smiled in relief. "Thank you. We'll take my car so we don't use up your gas." Grasping her hand, he kissed her palm.

She gently pried her hand from him. "But, Will, you have to understand that we can't be anything more than friends. I—I think you're a great guy, but I just don't have romantic feelings for you."

He couldn't hide his disappointment. "I understand. I'd obviously hoped for more, but I'm grateful for your friendship. I'll call you when I find out my appointment time."

Releasing her breath, Kat felt almost giddy. He hadn't taken it nearly as badly as she'd feared. "Yes, please do… Well, good night."

"Good night, Kat. Sleep well."

WILL STARED AT THE DOOR long after Kat closed it behind her. She was supposed to become his lover. Supposed to bond with him. Instead, she'd given him the let's-be-friends speech he'd heard so many times. He'd thought Kat would be different. But she was the same as all the rest.

The only difference now was that he was older and smarter. His plans would simply require minor adjustments.

He smiled.

After tomorrow, Kat and her money would be his. One way or the other.

TONY WAITED FOR KAT in the shadows, sitting on her front porch, feet propped on a second chair.

He knew he shouldn't be here, but he'd been restless after his online search produced a telephone listing for Mary Deveraux in a Chicago suburb. With the time difference, it was too late to call her tonight.

Time was running out; he could feel it. The new sense of urgency had as much to do with protecting Kat as to handling the Treadway case. That's why he was sitting here waiting for her to return from Will's suite rather than decoding Sterling's spreadsheet.

He fidgeted, itching to work.

Hearing shoes crunching on gravel, Tony hoped like hell Kat was by herself. His desire to hurt Will was strong tonight. If he was honest, he'd admit he was as angry at himself as at Will. It bothered him that he'd hurt Kat, when he'd only had the best intentions.

The footsteps slowed. "What are you doing here?" Kat asked.

"We need to talk." He stood, opting for the advantage of height. And hoping she'd invite him in.

Crossing her arms, she hardened her expression. "So talk. And make it quick."

"Can we go inside?"

"I'd swear I just had this conversation with Will. Don't you guys have any better way to get a woman into bed?"

Tony ignored the reference to Sterling, because to do otherwise would drive him crazy. "Scout's honor." He gave the Scout salute, hoping to at least elicit a smile from her.

She obviously wasn't in the mood to be humored. "I don't think so. Better hurry. I have an early day tomorrow."

He stepped closer to touch her.

She held up her hand. "Don't. You've got five minutes."

"You don't understand how dangerous Sterling is. He's…hurt people…in the past."

"I thought you might be here to straighten things out between us, maybe even apologize for being such a jerk. And allow me to finish a sentence and tell you I'd intended to let Will down gently at lunch today. Then, with the air cleared, you and I could see if there was something real going on with us. Something worth protecting. Obviously, I was wrong."

Her mouth trembled, but she recovered almost immediately. She raised her chin, staring him down.

It was important that he make her understand. Grasping her shoulders, he said, "I'm sorry I hurt you. You'll never know how sorry. But right now, your safety is the most important issue. You're not safe with Will. Stay away from him."

"Guess what, Tony? You don't get to choose my friends. I'm done. *You* stay away from *me*. Far, far away."

He held up his hands. "I had to try, Kat. I understand why you're pissed at me. But please don't put yourself in danger to spite me."

"Don't flatter yourself. You don't understand anything. Now get away from my door."

He'd handled this case badly from the start. All because he'd gotten emotionally involved and divided his focus.

Defeated, Tony turned and walked away.

KAT ALLOWED HERSELF the luxury of slamming the door behind her.

Of course, she could have told him Will knew her feelings were strictly platonic. But her pride wouldn't allow her to let Tony think he'd won.

Now who was playing games?

She wrapped her arms around herself yet again, as if she could hold in her pain. Not only had she shared her body with Tony, she'd shared all of her heart, even the pieces she'd held back from Zach.

Bending at the waist, she keened to herself. Nausea welled up, but she beat it back. If she kept the emotional carnage carefully contained, she could pretend it didn't exist.

Phoenix Rising, what a joke. This was supposed to be her time to heal, to move on. Oh, she'd moved on all right.

Kat went to the bathroom and splashed cool water on her face. Her reflection in the mirror above the sink showed huge, haunted eyes.

Swallowing hard, she gave in to the defeat dragging her down. She changed into her boxers and tank top and crawled into bed.

Tonight was for grieving her losses.

CHAPTER TWENTY-TWO

IN A FOUL MOOD, Tony returned to his casita after breakfast. Not only had he been unable to break Sterling's code despite hours of work last night, but Lorraine had informed him that Kat and Will were eating breakfast in his room.

It didn't take a brain surgeon to figure out Sterling was borrowing a page out of Ted Bundy's book. The serial killer had gained his victims' trust by wearing a fake cast and asking women for help. It was an effective ploy. Especially for someone as warmhearted as Kat. She seemed unable to resist a man who needed her.

The idea rankled. Tony's father had raised him to respect women, treat them as equals, yet always, always be ready to protect them. His mother had reinforced the rule. The Rangers had refined it.

Tony dialed Mary Deveraux's number and turned on the recording device.

He was in luck. A woman answered on the second ring.

"Mrs. Deveraux, my name is Randy Carlisle. I'm the hiring manager with World Corporation and a

Mr. William Powers gave your name as a personal reference…."

The pretext slipped easily off his tongue. Not because he enjoyed lying, but because it was necessary.

"I can't believe that man had the nerve to give my name as a reference. He's a cheat and a liar. If you hire him, he'll steal you blind."

"Oh, um, how unfortunate. He seemed on the level when I interviewed him."

"Of course he did. He'll tell you anything you want to hear, and he's very good at it."

Tony took notes on a spiral pad while she talked. Backup in case the recording failed.

"My boss will want me to give specific examples. Does one in particular come to mind?"

"What did you say your name was?"

"Ran—"

The line went dead.

Frustrated, Tony turned off the recording device. He was so close, yet couldn't nail anything down.

KAT SAT DOWN IN FRONT OF her laptop, still groggy despite two cups of coffee she'd brewed herself, and a short conversation with Will to bow out of breakfast in his suite.

Her eyes felt gritty and out of focus, her eyelids puffy from crying herself to sleep. Her restorative vacation left her feeling as if she'd been hit by a truck and emotionally drained.

Perfect. She could have stayed home and been miserable and saved herself a pile of money and even more heartache. Zach was starting to look like a real prize after her interactions with Tony and Will.

Booting up the computer, she checked her Web mail account. A forward from Annie inspired a wobbly smile. Then the usual spam and…an e-mail from her dad, received this morning. The subject line had been left blank.

She opened it and was surprised at the length. Her father mostly forwarded jokes or wrote only a few personal lines.

How bad could it be?

Dear Kat,
This e-mail is probably premature because there is so much I want to say to you, but I'm not yet healthy enough to tackle a full amends.

Kat absently sipped her coffee, afraid to read any further. He wasn't dying, but he apparently wasn't healthy, either. What if he had some sort of slow, wasting disease like ALS? Or a potentially fatal one, like AIDS?

She took a deep breath. Though she was vaguely aware of the phone ringing, she ignored it.

I haven't been in touch recently because I've been at a treatment center for recovering addicts.

What?

Kat set her cup down hard. The coffee sloshed to the rim.

There was no way her father was a drug addict.

This is very hard for me to admit to you. Who am I kidding? I wasn't able to admit it even to myself. I lied to you and to the other people I love to protect my secret. In the end, it was all that mattered.

I am a sex addict.

The bottom dropped out of Kat's world. Her mouth went dry. She tried desperately to regain the idea of her father as a drug addict. Because she could not accept that her dad was a pervert.

There was a knock at her door.

"Just a minute." Her voice was thin and high, as if the very life had been sucked from her, leaving behind the little girl who believed her father was a hero, even though he'd let her down time after time.

She scanned the rest of the e-mail, much of which didn't register. Something about twelve steps, a sponsor and a family visitation day she was invited to attend.

Slamming her laptop closed, Kat covered her mouth to subdue a hysterical laugh that made her eyes tear. The thought of visiting a sex addiction clinic with her stepmother, her mother, her sister and the new baby was so ludicrous, she couldn't believe it.

And yet she did.

Her laughter stopped.

"Kat, it's me, Will."

A kaleidoscope of memories clicked into place. Her father's late-night business emergencies, the hours he spent behind closed doors in his office, "filing reports." The awful fights with her mother, the divorce that was never explained. The different perfumes emanating from the clothes Kat had laundered for him after the divorce, along with strands of every hair color imaginable. The parade of women he'd dated before he'd married Sharon. The women Kat had suspected he'd dated after his remarriage.

The door handle rattled. "Kat, are you in there?"

Kat calmly walked to the door and opened it. The numbness she experienced was a welcome relief. "I'm sorry, I was in the bathroom."

"That's all? I thought I heard you crying. Or maybe laughing. It just didn't sound right."

"Everything's fine." And it was. Because she refused to believe her father was a sex addict. Even if it all finally added up.

Because she'd idolized her father.

"I'm fine. Really. What did you need?" She hoped he would leave soon, so she could quietly disintegrate without an audience.

"My appointment is at two-thirty. I thought maybe we'd leave early—say, noon? That way we could have lunch in town."

"That sounds fine. I'll see you then." She started to close the door, but Will stopped it with his hand.

"You're sure everything's okay? You seem…different. Kind of spacey."

There was no way she would confide this kind of information to Will. She could imagine how appalled he would be. Nice, neat Will wouldn't be able to comprehend relatives with nasty secrets like her father's.

TONY IGNORED THE call waiting tone on his cell as he jotted down the name of the software. He thanked John, his FBI contact—a young computer genius he'd worked with on a case when he was a Ranger—and ended the conversation.

Checking his missed calls, he saw his mom's number and realized he hadn't spoken to her in more than a week. He'd catch hell for sure. But it would have to wait awhile longer.

He rolled his shoulders to work out the kinks in his neck. Pulling up the Web site his colleague had recommended, he winced at the price of the decoding software. With his company still in the fledgling stages, he hesitated to lay out the money—and he certainly wouldn't charge the Treadways for it. But it was necessary.

Once the download was finished, he began the tedious chore of inputting the data from Will's spreadsheet. A knock at his door interrupted him when he was nearly done.

He was surprised to see Kat.

Not so surprised when she pushed her way into his room, turned and planted her hands on her hips.

"Please come in." Sarcasm could be such a great tool at times.

"You lied to me."

Uh-oh. "What do you mean?"

"You told me you were a good man, acting all stable and protective. But I saw through it. I knew you would only hurt me. I was very upfront about that. And what did you do?" she demanded.

"I imagine you're going to tell me."

"Damn straight. You pursued me. You kept after me, wore me down." She paced to the other room, stopping to pick up the wet towel he'd dropped on the floor.

He followed her, watching her go into the bathroom and arrange the towel over the shower rod.

"Housekeeping won't replace it if it's there. If the towel's on the floor, she brings me a new one."

Kat swiveled so fast it almost made him dizzy. She bore down on him, pointing. "Typical man. Expecting a woman to clean up your messes, then making up some story to cover your tracks."

Tony took a step back. He'd come up against some scary people in his day, but Kat spitting fire was damn impressive.

"Darlin', I don't understand a word you're saying. Are you okay?"

That seemed to infuriate her even more. "I wish you guys would quit asking me if I'm okay. I'm not the hysterical female type."

"I didn't say you were."

She advanced on him, poking his chest. "And then

you act all innocent, saying you're sorry for lying. As if that's going to make things better."

Something wasn't right here. He hadn't apologized, though he probably would if it didn't require endangering his case. Could this be another of those times when her upset had nothing to do with him?

Tears sparkled in her eyes. "Next you'll enter some damn twelve-step program, say you're sorry for screwing up my life…and invite me to visit on family day."

Tony took a chance and wrapped his arms around her. "Hey, what's this all about?"

She struggled, but his instincts told him to hold on. His response must've been right, because she stilled after a moment.

"Nothing." Her answer was muffled with her face pressed to his chest. Judging from the way her shoulders shook, and an occasional sniffle, she seemed to be having an all-out cry.

"Okay, nothing's wrong." He rubbed her back, tilting his head and closing his eyes at the pleasure of having her in his arms again. It didn't matter that he had no clue what had upset her.

After several minutes, she pulled back, wiping her eyes. His T-shirt was damp from her tears.

"I—I'm sorry."

"For what?"

"For going off on you like that."

Her hair curled wildly around her face. He brushed it away from her forehead. "I kind of enjoyed it."

She smacked him on the biceps with her open hand. "You would."

Sighing, he picked at a curl and rubbed it between his thumb and forefinger. He loved her tangle of red hair and wanted to see it on his pillow every morning. But it wasn't something he could offer her. At least not until he closed this case.

Raising her chin with his finger, he met her gaze. "What brought this on?"

She tried to glance away. "I—I don't know."

He smiled encouragingly, treasuring every minute with her. "Now who's lying?"

Stepping away from him, she returned to the front room, Tony on her heels. Once there, she faced him.

"My father is a sex addict."

Her bald statement hit him between the eyes. What could he say to a revelation like that?

"Whoa, that wasn't what I expected to hear."

"See? I knew you wouldn't understand." She stalked to the door, but he got there first, bracing his hand behind her head to keep the door shut.

"I didn't say I didn't understand. I said it wasn't what I expected to hear. I take it this came as a surprise?"

"What do you think?" She stared up at him.

"I think…addiction is hard on families. I've seen what it's done to guys I've worked with. I've seen it take over the lives of wives who couldn't handle the reality of being married to a cop."

Kat's eyes widened and he realized his mistake. Or

maybe on some level he had deliberately chosen Kat above duty.

"You're a cop."

There didn't seem to be much point in trying to talk his way out of this. Not when she'd come here accusing him of lying. "I'm a retired Texas Ranger. I operate my own private investigation firm. That part was the truth."

"I can't believe this." Her body tensed. "Is there anything men don't lie about?"

She wedged her hands against his chest and shoved hard.

He fell back a step to give her room, so she wouldn't feel trapped by his frame. "I couldn't tell you the truth. I'm on a case."

"Save me the explanations." Her disgust was evident in the downward tilt of her mouth. "I don't know where the lies end and the truth begins."

"Kat."

She sidestepped his halfhearted attempt to reach out to her. "The sad part is I really don't care anymore."

Watching the spark in her eyes fade to disillusionment was one of the hardest things he'd ever done.

"If you don't believe anything else I say, please, *please* believe that Will Sterling is dangerous."

"More dangerous than you? I don't think so."

She turned and walked out of his casita without a backward glance.

CHAPTER TWENTY-THREE

KAT RAN A BRUSH through her hair, secured it with a ponytail holder, applied lip gloss and was ready to go to Jasper with Will.

She was determined for forget all about Tony Perez and this crummy vacation.

Her laptop mocked her from the table.

It had taken guts for her father to send that e-mail. She couldn't imagine having to admit something so shameful to your child.

She at least owed him a response. Pulling it up, she hit Reply.

Dad, I don't understand much of this, but I love you no matter what. I'll be in touch soon. Love, Kat.

Biting her lip, she hit the send button before she lost her nerve.

Then she came to another decision. This vacation simply wasn't working for her. It was time to go home. After she brought Will back from the doctor's visit in Jasper, she would find Linda and settle her account.

She closed her laptop and placed it in her backpack, along with her new journal.

Pulling her suitcase out of the closet, Kat flipped it open. Her step was quick as she hauled her clothes from the dresser and closet to pile them on the bed. Then she started meticulously folding.

There was a knock at her door and she opened it, hoping it wasn't Tony, here to make more dire predictions.

"Oh, it's you, Will." Kat flinched at the disappointment in her voice.

Talk about lying to herself. She'd wanted it to be Tony. Wanted him to convince her he loved her more than anything, that he would never lie to her again. He would slip a diamond solitaire on her left ring finger, then follow by telling her the Perez men were ridiculously fertile and he intended to make lots of babies with her, starting immediately…

Kat smiled wistfully.

Blinking, she focused on the man in front of her.

"I'm sorry, I'm in a bad mood and I was caught off guard." She glanced at her watch. "You're a few minutes early."

He smiled. "I couldn't wait a moment longer to see you."

"Come in while I grab my purse and key card."

She turned, listening to the awkward rattle of his crutches. Poor guy just couldn't seem to catch a break.

Kat leaned into the bathroom, intent on turning off

the light. She saw her towel draped precisely over the shower rod.

She whipped it off and dropped it on the floor, kicking it into the corner.

Turning, she was startled to find Will behind her. She hadn't heard his crutches. Goose bumps rose on her arms.

Forcing a laugh, she said, "You scared me."

His smile was tender, as open as the desert outside. "Are you ready for our adventure?"

"Um, yes." Her cheeks flushed as she switched off the light.

They walked back through the bedroom. "Why the suitcase?" He nodded toward the bed.

For some reason, Kat was hesitant to confide in him. "I'm thinking of cutting my stay short. Some…family stuff has come up."

His mouth tightened. She could almost feel tension crackling between them.

"I had hoped we would have longer," he said.

The feeling wasn't mutual. And the more time she spent with Will, the more she felt something was…off. It wasn't anything she could put her finger on. Maybe Tony's warnings were affecting her more than she'd thought. But her gut insisted he was right.

"I had hoped so, too," she lied. "Let's exchange e-mail addresses and keep in touch." Another lie.

And Will must have sensed it, because his mouth thinned.

"You look angry," she said.

"Disappointed." He propped his crutches against the wet bar. "I thought it would be easy with you. But we can do things the hard way."

"I don't understand."

"No, I'm sure you don't. Did you tell anyone you were taking me to the doctor this afternoon?"

"I...don't think so." She'd actually mentioned it in passing to Lorraine, but decided not to tell Will that. She was getting a weird vibe from him.

Pulling her cell phone out of her purse, Kat flipped it open. "As a matter of fact, I think I'll let Linda know in case she's looking for me."

"I'll take that." Will wrenched the phone away from her and pocketed it.

"Hey—"

"I don't want to hurt you, Kat."

She almost snorted in disbelief until she saw the pistol in his hand. He must have had it in the pocket of his windbreaker.

"What are you doing?"

"Sit down at the table." He jerked his head toward the dining nook.

Her thoughts raced as she complied. This was bad, very bad. "I've got money and credit cards in my purse. I'll give you my personal identification number."

"Yes, you will. But that can wait till we get on the road." He pulled a sheaf of papers from inside his windbreaker. "This is my insurance policy, in case something goes wrong and we get separated. Or you do something stupid and I'm forced to kill you."

Kat swallowed hard. How could she have been so wrong about this man? "I'll cooperate. Whatever you want."

"That's what I like to hear." He caressed her cheek with his left hand, before fishing a plastic tie-strap out of his pants. "Secure your left wrist to the chair rail. I'll check to make sure it's tight."

She did what he said, which wasn't easy because her hands shook.

"Good." He placed the papers on the table in front of her, smoothing the folds. "General power of attorney."

"I can read." Her terse response was as automatic as it was sarcastic.

Her head snapped to the side when Will backhanded her across her cheek. Her eyes teared, her ears rang. She shook her head to clear it. He was going to pay for that.

She controlled her breathing, allowed her mouth to tremble. "I'll sign it."

"Excellent."

Tony couldn't think straight after Kat left. It was as if he'd been dropped in an alien land where he didn't know the rules.

Becoming a Ranger had been easy compared to this. There were strict guidelines and rules he was required to follow. There were also gray areas he'd learned to navigate with the guidance of his partner, a veteran agent.

With Kat, everything seemed to be a gray area and there were no veterans to help him navigate. His marriage to Corinne hadn't seemed to clue him in, either. Besides, he'd ultimately failed with her. She hadn't wanted to go the distance to repair what they'd once had.

He couldn't see Kat giving up on a marriage without a fight. Hell, she'd gotten in his face about a vacation fling less than a week old.

Phrasing it like that made him feel like a total jerk. What had developed between them was way more than a fling, no matter how many times he denied it.

Tony's stomach grumbled. Glancing at his watch, he realized it was time for lunch. He should stay and work through the rest of the data entry, but knew he would never concentrate. Maybe he could talk to Kat at the dining room, find a way to get through to her.

His cell phone rang as he was heading out the door. The display showed a number that was vaguely familiar, so he picked up.

"Randy Carlisle, I presume?" It was a woman's voice.

"Who's calling, please?" He had a pretty good idea, but needed to get his wits about him.

"Mary Deveraux, of course. I want to know why you're looking for information on Bill Powers."

He briefly thought of trying another pretext, but decided against it. "My name is Tony Perez. I'm a private investigator and I suspect Bill Powers also goes by the name Will Sterling. I'm afraid he's trying to con a...

female friend of mine. She recently came into some money."

"Get your friend away from him as fast as you can. Not only did he trick me into signing a power of attorney form, he also took out a life insurance policy in my name. If my niece hadn't practically kidnapped me, I'm afraid something really bad might have happened. As it is, he stole hundreds of thousands of dollars."

"Did you inform the authorities, ma'am?"

"The police took a report, but said they hit a dead end. I think they were too short-handed because of budget cuts to do a proper investigation…. And I was too embarrassed and ashamed to press them. Seeing him again brought it all back. Now I'm mad. He's stolen my trust in people and in my own instincts. Calling you is my way of taking back my life."

"Thank you, ma'am. May I call you later if I need further information?"

"You certainly may. But please use your own name, Mr. Perez."

"I will."

Clicking off the call, he grabbed his wallet and keys, heading for the dining room at a jog.

It took all of Tony's self-control to slow to a walk as he reached the building. He stood at the entrance, scanning the crowd. He couldn't see the beacon of Kat's hair, or hear her voice.

"Hello, Tony." Lorraine smiled as she and Lola came in behind him. "She's not here."

"What?" He was too distracted to catch what she'd said.

"Kat's not here. She drove Will into town for a doctor's appointment."

Now Lorraine had his attention. "How long ago?"

"She said they were leaving at noon, and would eat lunch on the way."

Glancing at his watch, Tony swore under his breath. It was twelve-fifteen.

"Lorraine, I'm afraid Will might hurt her. I believe he takes advantage of vulnerable women."

Lola gasped.

"I knew it!" Lorraine's triumph quickly turned to concern. "Poor Kat."

"I'm going to check her room and see if she's still there. I need you to call the sheriff and ask him to meet me out here. Tell him I'm Texas Department of Public Safety, retired. Then find Linda and let her know what's going on."

Lola's eyes widened. "You're a Ranger?"

Her sister grinned. "I had you pegged for law enforcement. I'll make that call. Now go and help Kat."

He nodded and ran outside, lengthening his stride. He dodged around the honeymooning couple, who appeared to be having their first fight in the middle of the path.

Tony's chest burned, not from altitude or exertion, but because he was terrified for Kat. He couldn't imagine a world without her smart-ass comments or the vulnerability they protected. And the knowledge that if she loved him the way he loved her, she would always fight for their relationship with everything she had. Kat wasn't a quitter.

She would never allow them to grow apart over the years. No, she'd be in his face at the first sign of trouble, forcing him to be the kind of husband he had never been for Corrine. And maybe, just maybe, together they would succeed where he had failed before.

He needed to think like a hard-edged cop right now, not Kat's lover. There would be plenty of time later to fall apart once she was safe.

At least he hoped he would have plenty of time with Kat later.

Tony slowed as he approached her casita. The shutters in front appeared closed, but could have been cracked enough for Sterling to peer out.

Or he might be too late, and Kat had left with Will.

KAT WAS SURPRISED HER life didn't flash before her eyes as Will held the gun pressed against her temple. Instead, she saw the puckered newborn face of the niece or nephew she would never know. How could she toss away the opportunity to see the birth of Nicole's baby simply because it made her ache over her own losses, her own mistakes?

"Sign it."

The gun warmed to her body heat. How strange. She'd thought it would remain cold.

Kat did as she was told, signing slowly, as if this

last signature had to be perfect. The implication was terrifying.

She'd wasted so much time trying to reach a perfection that was impossible. Bouncing from one extreme to another in an attempt to earn love: braniac to high school temptress to driven CPA; devoted daughter to rescuer of bad boys. All that seeking had left her... empty.

She'd thought her time at Phoenix Rising had been wasted, but now she realized small changes had been taking place. Changes in her perception of herself. And during her times with Tony, the hollow ache inside had disappeared, as if suddenly she was enough just the way she was.

Will's voice sounded deceptively normal when he said, "Very good. Fortunately, a fictitious witness signature and notary seal can be bought. Now fold them as they were."

"With one hand?" She raised an eyebrow.

"I have confidence in you."

Right. He wouldn't risk setting down the gun. Kat managed to refold the document.

He tucked it inside his jacket.

"Now that I have my insurance policy, we're going for a little drive. I've leased a hunting cabin near Payson. Very remote...secluded." He brushed her cheek with his fingertips. "We'll see if you and I can come to an understanding. We'll consider it our honeymoon."

Kat's mouth went dry. "And if we don't come to an

understanding?" It was a hypothetical question. Because she had a fair idea of the answer.

"Then you will no longer be useful. And I'm sure neither of us wants that."

"No, we don't." Kat couldn't let him take her from this room. Once they were on the road, he would find a secluded spot to kill her, and nobody would ever know what had happened.

"Am I taking this chair with me?" she asked, pointing to her left hand, tied to the rail.

"That's one of the things I like about you, Kat—your sense of humor. You can be quite entertaining as well as beautiful."

He produced a pocket knife and cut the plastic tie.

Kat tried to catalog the contents of the room to determine the best weapon. Tilting her head to look up at him, she noticed a glint of aluminum out of the corner of her eye. They would walk by the wet bar on their way to the door....

"I want you to slowly and carefully move toward the door. If you do anything stupid, I'll shoot you."

"I understand." Kat rose, her heart pounding. She would have only one chance.

Staring straight ahead, she walked toward the exit. One step, two.

Kat hit the ground and rolled to the bar, grasping a crutch and swinging it with all her might.

A deafening shot exploded from Will's gun at the same time the crutch connected with his knees, bringing him down. The force of the blow reverberated through the aluminum and up her arms.

Glass shattered everywhere as a body came crashing through the Arcadia door, tucked and rolled, then sprang upright.

Tony.

"Don't move, Sterling." Tony carried his own pistol and it was aimed at Will's head.

Though her ears rang, Kat could hear pounding on the door. "Sheriff! Open up!"

The pistol had been knocked out of Will's hand, but he groped wildly for it.

Kat watched for a moment, feeling strangely detached. Then a single thought worked its way through her fog. If Will reached the weapon, he would shoot Tony.

Jumping to her feet, Kat stepped on Will's wrist, grinding her heel down as hard as she could. The sickening crunch of breaking bone made her wince. But she didn't ease the pressure until the front door banged open and the sheriff took control of the situation.

Kat started shaking all over as the sheriff handcuffed Will where he lay on the floor, unable to stand. The paramedics later told them his kneecaps might be broken.

Tony holstered his weapon and Kat walked into his arms.

IT WAS HOURS BEFORE Tony could be alone with Kat. There were statements to make, friends to reassure….

Lola, Lorraine, Brooke and Garth had finally left Tony's casita, prodded by Linda, who closed the door on her way out.

Now it was just the two of them, nestled together on the couch.

Tony cradled Kat's head against his shoulder. "I was afraid he'd hurt you. Afraid I might lose you."

She glanced up, her smile soft. It warmed him through and through. "I know."

"I'm not going away. You're stuck with me. If you're still hung up about my cover—"

"Lie."

"Okay, lie. I'll just have to take the next sixty years or so to prove how trustworthy I am." He rubbed her arm, wondering how he'd lived without her the first forty years of his life.

The remaining tension eased from her body.

Sighing, she said, "Sometimes I may need that extra reassurance. And if you're going to hang around that long, I guess I'll have to learn to compromise, too."

"Yeah, probably."

"And where are these sixty years going to take place?"

He'd decided nothing was going to keep him away from Kat—not distance, not family, not career. "I haven't had a chance to think that far ahead. I'm sure we can figure it out together."

"I imagine we can…. I've always wanted to see more of Texas."

"You have?" He tipped her chin up with his finger. Her expression reassured him.

Still, he needed to make sure they were on the same page. "We'll want to stick around the Phoenix area at least until your sister's baby is born."

"Absolutely. And after that?"

"Then, I'm hoping you have enough vacation time left for that trip to Texas. My family will be dying to meet you. I'll have a lot of explaining to do to my mom. She'll be pissed if she thinks I kept you a secret."

Kat laughed. "Sounds like a kindred soul. How long a vacation do I need?"

"Whoa, back up a minute. I've never thought of you being like my mom…but now that you mention it, I think you're every bit as feisty as she is." He shuddered.

Kat poked him in his ribs, hard. "What do you mean, feisty?"

"I think you just answered your own question." He rubbed his side.

"I'm sure I'll love your mother."

"I'm sure she'll love you almost as much as I do." Tony kissed her, enjoying the familiar taste of peppermint and Kat.

"You never answered my question. How long a vacation do I need for Texas?"

"As long as possible. I have a lot of family—my mom, two brothers and a zillion aunts, uncles and cousins."

"Would two weeks do it?" He heard a smile in her voice.

"Might be cutting it close, but we'll manage. And you'll need to save vacation time for the wedding."

"Whose wedding?"

"Ours, of course."

They lapsed into silence. It took all of Tony's self-control to wait her out.

Another minute went by before she fidgeted again. Then she pulled away from him and straightened. "This is one of those times I need reassurance. A woman doesn't want ambiguous references to love and marriage. There is a certain protocol."

He clasped her hands in his. "I love you, Kat. Totally and completely. Will you marry me?"

He began to doubt himself when she gazed up at him, frowning.

"What have I said wrong now?"

Her fingers were petal-soft as she traced the line of his jaw. "I need to be sure of something first. Was it only your case that made you pull away from me?"

Crap. She wanted him to dig deep and reveal stuff he'd rather keep to himself.

Slowly, he smiled, because that was one of the things he loved about her. She made him dig deep. He could do this. He could be man enough to embarrass the shit out of himself. "My case was a big part of it. But I was afraid of…loving you so much, only to grow apart. Of waking up one day to find out all of a sudden you were unhappy and pissed and wanted a divorce. That's how it happened with Corrine…."

Kat crossed her arms over her chest.

"But when you came to my room this morning to read me the riot act again," he continued, "I knew you'd never sit back and let a problem become so big we couldn't solve it. You'd get right in my face and we'd hash it out, find a solution and move on. What I'm trying to say is that you won't allow me to fail at another marriage. I don't have to worry about not doing it right, because you'll guide me, maybe sometimes even bully me, into being the best husband."

Kat smiled, tears trickling down her face. She threw her arms around him and hugged him tightly. "I love you, Tony, and I would be honored to be your wife. Though I do resent being called a bully."

Kissing the top of her head, he closed his eyes, amazed at his luck.

But then he had to ask, "You don't think I'm a bad guy anymore, do you?"

She pulled away to look at him. "No, you're not bad. You do kind of scare me sometimes, though, because you want me for who I am. But you don't need me."

He pressed his finger to her lips. "Oh, you've got me all wrong. I need you way more than you will probably ever know."

EPILOGUE

KAT'S FATHER WAITED, his hand extended expectantly. He was handsome in his morning coat.

Gathering her ivory train, she grasped his hand as he helped her down from the vintage Western carriage, pulled by a draft horse with tea roses and ribbons woven in its mane.

It was a gorgeous September day and the meadow near Phoenix Rising was alive with Indian summer. The sun warmed them, laughter abounded among their guests, and high above, a red-tailed hawk circled.

Her father's eyes shone suspiciously bright. "Thank you for allowing me to be a part of your special day."

"You're going to make me cry, Dad." She sniffled, hoping her makeup wouldn't run. But it would be worth it.

She straightened his cravat, her fingers shaking.

He stilled her hand. "You don't need to fix me any-more, Kit-Kat. Today, I intend to be the father you deserve. Now let's go get you married."

She stood on tiptoe to kiss his cheek, then smoothed the single tear away with her thumb. "I'm proud of you."

He offered her his arm, standing even taller, if it was possible.

Slipping her hand in the crook of his elbow, Kat thought she couldn't have asked for a better wedding gift.

She had thought her life might flash before her eyes when she was held at gunpoint, but it hadn't. It happened now as she walked down the runner in their special meadow, where she and Tony had shared s'mores months earlier. Seeing the faces of family and friends lining both sides made her realize how fortunate they were.

Newer friends like Lola and Lorraine, sitting next to the Fremonts. At the front, near the minister, stood longtime friends like matron of honor Annie Marsh Vincent, and Kat's sister, Nicole, as an attendant. Because Tony didn't want to cause hard feelings by choosing one brother over the other, Annie's husband, Drew, had agreed to stand in as best man, his uniform impressive. Tony's brothers made handsome groomsmen. But not nearly as handsome as the groom, who straightened his vest, fidgeting until the bridal march began.

When Tony looked up and their gazes connected, Kat knew she had come home.

* * * * *

COMING NEXT MONTH

Available October 12, 2010

#1662 THE GOOD PROVIDER
Spotlight on Sentinel Pass
Debra Salonen

#1663 THE SCANDAL AND CARTER O'NEILL
The Notorious O'Neills
Molly O'Keefe

#1664 ADOPTED PARENTS
Suddenly a Parent
Candy Halliday

#1665 CALLING THE SHOTS
You, Me & the Kids
Ellen Hartman

#1666 THAT RUNAWAY SUMMER
Return to Indigo Springs
Darlene Gardner

#1667 DANCE WITH THE DOCTOR
Single Father
Cindi Myers

LARGER-PRINT BOOKS!

GET 2 FREE LARGER-PRINT NOVELS PLUS
2 FREE GIFTS!

HARLEQUIN®

Super Romance

Exciting, emotional, unexpected!

YES! Please send me 2 FREE LARGER-PRINT Harlequin® Superromance® novels and my 2 FREE gifts (gifts are worth about $10). After receiving them, if I don't wish to receive any more books, I can return the shipping statement marked "cancel." If I don't cancel, I will receive 6 brand-new novels every month and be billed just $5.44 per book in the U.S. or $5.99 per book in Canada. That's a saving of at least 13% off the cover price! It's quite a bargain! Shipping and handling is just 50¢ per book.* I understand that accepting the 2 free books and gifts places me under no obligation to buy anything. I can always return a shipment and cancel at any time. Even if I never buy another book from Harlequin, the two free books and gifts are mine to keep forever.

139/339 HDN E5PS

Name _____ (PLEASE PRINT) _____

Address _____ Apt. # _____

City _____ State/Prov. _____ Zip/Postal Code _____

Signature (if under 18, a parent or guardian must sign) _____

Mail to the **Harlequin Reader Service:**
IN U.S.A.: P.O. Box 1867, Buffalo, NY 14240-1867
IN CANADA: P.O. Box 609, Fort Erie, Ontario L2A 5X3

Not valid for current subscribers to Harlequin Superromance Larger-Print books.

**Are you a current subscriber to Harlequin Superromance books
and want to receive the larger-print edition?
Call 1-800-873-8635 today!**

* Terms and prices subject to change without notice. Prices do not include applicable taxes. N.Y. residents add applicable sales tax. Canadian residents will be charged applicable provincial taxes and GST. Offer not valid in Quebec. This offer is limited to one order per household. All orders subject to approval. Credit or debit balances in a customer's account(s) may be offset by any other outstanding balance owed by or to the customer. Please allow 4 to 6 weeks for delivery. Offer available while quantities last.

Your Privacy: Harlequin Books is committed to protecting your privacy. Our Privacy Policy is available online at www.eHarlequin.com or upon request from the Reader Service. From time to time we make our lists of customers available to reputable third parties who may have a product or service of interest to you. If you would prefer we not share your name and address, please check here. ☐

Help us get it right—We strive for accurate, respectful and relevant communications. To clarify or modify your communication preferences, visit us at www.ReaderService.com/consumerchoice.

HSRLP10R

HARLEQUIN®

A *Romance*

FOR EVERY MOOD™

Spotlight on

Inspirational

Wholesome romances
that touch the heart and soul.

See the next page
to enjoy a sneak peek from
the Love Inspired® inspirational series.

*See below for a sneak peek at
our inspirational line, Love Inspired®.
Introducing HIS HOLIDAY BRIDE
by bestselling author Jillian Hart*

Autumn Granger gave her horse rein to slide toward the town's new sheriff.

"Hey, there." The man in a brand-new Stetson, black T-shirt, jeans and riding boots held up a hand in greeting. He stepped away from his four-wheel drive with "Sheriff" in black on the doors and waded through the grasses. "I'm new around here."

"I'm Autumn Granger."

"Nice to meet you, Miss Granger. I'm Ford Sherman, from Chicago." He knuckled back his hat, revealing the most handsome face she'd ever seen. Big blue eyes contrasted with his sun-tanned complexion.

"I'm guessing you haven't seen much open land. Out here, you've got to keep an eye on cows or they're going to tear your vehicle apart."

"What?" He whipped around. Sure enough, mammoth black-and-white creatures had started to gnaw on his four-wheel drive. They clustered like a mob, mouths and tongues and teeth bent on destruction. One cow tried to pry the wiper off the windshield, another chewed on the side mirror. Several leaned through the open window, licking the seats.

"Move along, little dogie." He didn't know the first thing about cattle.

The entire herd swiveled their heads to study him curiously. Not a single hoof shifted. The animals soon returned to chewing, licking, digging through his possessions.

Autumn laughed, a warm and wonderful sound. "Thanks,

I needed that." She then pulled a bag from behind her saddle and waved it at the cows. "Look what I have, guys. Cookies."

Cows swung in her direction, and dozens of liquid brown eyes brightened with cookie hopes. As she circled the car, the cattle bounded after her. The earth shook with the force of their powerful hooves.

"Next time, you're on your own, city boy." She tipped her hat. The cowgirl stayed on his mind, the sweetest thing he had ever seen.

Will Ford be able to stick it out in the country
to find out more about Autumn?
Find out in HIS HOLIDAY BRIDE
by bestselling author Jillian Hart,
available in October 2010
only from Love Inspired®.

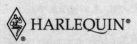